"Let Me Be Yours"

M/M Gay Romance

David Horne

This book is intended for Adults (ages 18+) only. The contents may be offensive to some readers. It may contain graphic language, explicit sexual content, and adult situations. May contain scenes of unprotected sex. Please do not read this book if you are offended by content as mentioned above or if you are under the age of 18.

Please educate yourself on safe sex practices before making potentially life-changing decisions about sex in real life. If you're not sure where to start, see here: http://www.jerrycoleauthor.com/safe-sex-resources/ (courtesy of Jerry Cole).

This story is a work of fiction. Names, characters, businesses, places, events and incidents are the products of the author's imagination or used in a fictitious manner and are not to be construed as real. Any resemblance to actual persons, living or dead, or actual events is purely coincidental. Products or brand names mentioned are trademarks of their respective holders or companies. The cover uses licensed images and are shown for illustrative purposes only. Any person(s) that may be depicted on the cover are simply models.

Edition v1.00 (2020.06.21)

http://www.DavidHorneauthor.com

Special thanks to the following volunteer readers who helped with proofreading: Bob, RB, JayBee, Big Kid, Jennie O., and those who assisted but wished to be anonymous. Thank you so much for your support.

Chapter One

Lucas Lopes

Standing in the high dormitory window on a foggy day, you could almost feel as though you were in the clouds. I liked to pretend that it was true, that the world below me was getting farther and farther away. Things were easier in the sky, and I didn't have to look down at the same grass and concrete I'd known my whole young life.

In the clouds I could pretend this wasn't where I grew up, could pretend I'd had my choice of schools, instead of ending up in this one as a matter of convenience and poverty. I could also, mercifully, blow smoke out the window and no one would notice. It was a bad habit, I knew, even back when I started it. But this place, the place on which I'm quick to blame everything, breeds bad habits. They're the only thing you can turn to when you're forced to live on the muddy ground of my New York State town. And I took it with me into the foggy sky like a reminder that I would eventually have to go back down.

And sometimes, as I stood there soaring through the atmosphere, the fog would clear. I would come in for a landing and put my cigarette out on the windowsill, thanking God or whomever that you didn't have to put a security deposit down on a dorm room. You just paid up front, a surprisingly handsome fee for a state school. This allowed you to leave your dents and stains and burn marks. Then they paid someone to come in, paint over it, buff it out, and make it shine like new for the next student to ruin it all over again.

It was a bit like my old bedroom back home, which was not far away. I'd not been out of the house three days by the time my mother tossed the old twin-sized mattress out into the street for free, by the time she stripped the wallpaper and waxed the floors. She'd always wanted a guest room. I had, with great haste, been demoted to 'guest.' I could have just adopted that new title over the summer, stayed in the freshly painted guest room in a bed that no longer held my lanky shape. I could have been grown up about it and suffered through one last summer of feeling like anyone could own me, and then left my mother's house with my middle finger in the air.

But I didn't. I stayed in the sweaty basement of a friend's house, hedging my bets as to whether she and I would hate each other by the end of it. I guess we were lucky.

I'd left Angela's house a week before the official move-in day, desperate for any amount of time alone I could get my hands on, after two months of family dinners and the sound of the television, turned way up for her father's slowly failing ears. It had been six days since I got to the dorm, but still my stuff lay unpacked in a disorganized heap, items taken out as-needed from the sloppy pyramid of suitcases and boxes. It was something I ought to fix, given that my roommate would be getting in today. As juniors, we were finally lucky enough to have some semblance of actual floor space between our beds. It was a scratchy blue carpet no one could ever quite get the smell of spilled beer out of, but it was a luxury I'd not had since coming to this school.

This time, when the fog cleared, that clarity was met with the ever-jarring sound of a train, warning everyone of its arrival. It was a sound I'd been hearing since birth, that same whistle, the same ringing of the descending barrier to keep cars off the tracks. The train station was right across the road from campus, and only a few miles from my old house. Behind it there lay an old factory made of bricks, with a high smokestack and hundreds of little cracks in the windows. It was some of the remaining evidence that this town was a hotbed of decay. Everything else was in a state of repair or had already been fixed up into something that no longer resembled the crumbling economy. The school had been too.

Northeast State College used to, back in the 1920s, be known as Greystone Psychiatric Hospital. Its sprawling campus climbed well into the base of the mountain, all brick buildings and cobblestone pathways. A place to heal or get a lobotomy, depending on how much trouble you caused. Once it was shut down, all patients released into the world untreated, it quickly fell into disrepair. Until the late 80s it was nothing but the source of ghost stories and a place to sneak in and prove to your friends that you weren't chicken.

But now its halls were full of a different kind of insanity: the unbearable mental anguish of being something akin to an adult for the very first time.

The train came in, slowing to its screeching stop. Through the dirty windows I could see the silhouettes. It was a mostly-empty train, always, because all the worthwhile stops came before this one. The only people riding the train this far upstate at ten in the morning were winos returning from the city, or students doomed to move into the dorms without the help of an SUV or their parents.

And so, the first time I saw him was from above. The faraway approximation of a sandy-haired young man, laden with a backpack and wheeling along a suitcase behind him. Though I could not make out the detail of his face, though I could not see him well enough to make any sort of judgment, I felt immediately like a voyeur. Like looking at him was a depraved act, like he was something I was not supposed to see.

It was a feeling I'd not had in a long time. It felt like that old first inkling that I was attracted to men, seeing them, and getting the sense that whatever the flutter was I felt in my chest, was different than any other sensation. Realizing that not every boy around me felt that same excitement.

But something about the vague, far-off shape of him sent through me that old familiar thrill. I quickly shook it off, knowing that in my near-constant mild depression I was likely to fall in love with every handsome stranger for a while. But imagining a life with him that might save me, I knew wasn't the way to be saved. I was supposed to save myself, but it would just be so much easier if someone else did it for me. I would, I told myself, never see this guy again, unless we somehow ended up in a class together.

I turned away from the window then and sighed at my massive pile of unpacked belongings. Running one skinny hand through my grown-out hair, smoothing down the knots and flyaways I'd allowed it to collect, I set about trying to make this place look a little bit more like someone actually lived in it.

I unzipped the suitcase with most of my clothes in it, all stuffed in at random, wrinkled from the haphazard packing. It seemed to explode with an impossible volume of thrift-store shirts and unpaired socks. It went into the dresser in the very same fashion, but at least it was no longer in the suitcase. I set the record player on my desk, lined my sneakers up in a row on the floor. In one of my mislabeled shoeboxes, I found the little rainbow flag, the desk ornament Angela's mother had bought me in an attempt to show her approval. I twirled it between my fingers, watching the blur of colors whip around, contemplating if I ought to display it.

The reactions from previous roommates had been varied. They ranged from indifference to obvious discomfort. There was no telling what this new guy might think. And though I knew I ought not to care, that I ought to live my life out loud like so many people had told me to, still I hesitated. It was so very important, then, to be liked.

But as I held the little flag in my hand, I heard the struggle of a key in a lock, and the turning of a metal handle. I turned around, my hand still wrapped around the stick of the flag, and I saw him for the second time. The guy from the train station, a sheen of sweat on his forehead.

Wonderful, I thought, that his first impression of me should be this. Standing disheveled in sweatpants, holding a pride flag like I was reluctantly standing on a float in a god damn parade. I gulped, slammed the ornament down on the surface of my desk, and attempted to smile. He smiled back, immediately establishing his capability to absolve me. It was a wide, tired grin, the kind someone has when they've finally, after much struggle, reached a place where they can settle down their load and breathe. With a happy groan, he let the backpack slide from off his shoulder, and tossed his head back. He was tall, like me, but looked a lot sturdier. His arms radiated strength, more toned than my own skinny limbs, and his clothes seemed to fit him more properly than they ought. I felt then not only like a voyeur, but very ugly.

But still he was smiling, reaching out a hand for me to shake. Absolved, again.

"Are you Lucas?" he asked me, the kind of question you ask even though you already know the answer but are still deathly afraid of being wrong. I nodded.

He introduced himself as Ryan, and I noticed in him the slightest hint of a Southern accent. Buried deep as if he was trying to keep it a secret.

He threw his suitcase up on his bed and dragged an arm across his forehead to wipe away the sweat. It had rendered his hair all stringy, but somehow, he didn't look like a mess. Some men were made to sweat and be strong.

I soon found out that my hearing wasn't tricking me. He came from South Carolina, a transfer student from a two-year community college program. He'd long dreamed of coming up to New York and had made a deal with his father that if he got a 4.0, he was free to travel wherever he pleased.

"I got the grades," he told me as he neatly stacked his pants into a dresser drawer. "But celebrated a little too hard. N' he said to me 'New York? Have it your way,' so that's why I'm here instead of the city." He laughed, and I laughed, but then his face took on a distinct look of guilt. "I'm sorry man, not trying to say this place is--"

"A shit hole?" I interrupted, waving a hand. "It's fine, because you're right." More genuine but as-yet uncertain laughter.

As we continued to unpack, we set about the usual questions. What's your major, what's your plan. He told me he was an English major, and my head was filled with the idea that I was now rooming with

William Fucking Faulkner, but then he told me his focus was on poetry. Another thing his father punished him for.

"How about you?" he asked me, and I wondered if he wanted to know, or was simply following a script.

"Journalism."

"Oh, *America's most wanted*," he said, and pointed his fingers at me as if shooting two pistols. "Careful out there, bud."

With great relief that he was apparently not a staunch conservative, I put the little rainbow flag in with the cup full of pens on my desk. If he saw it, he didn't say anything.

And unfortunately, one's sexuality is not part of the script. What's your major? Do you have siblings? Who do you fuck? It just doesn't come up naturally. I felt very much like an investigative journalist indeed, during that first meeting. Trying to glean the details of him, the nuances, without actually having to ask. But I wasn't particularly good at my job. Still, I learned a lot of other things about him. His family owned the largest farm in South Carolina, and his parents tended to hoard their wealth. He'd spent his summer as he spent every summer since he was strong enough to lift a bale of hay, working on the farm in exchange for the ongoing privilege of getting to live in that giant farmhouse.

"My house is just up the road," I admitted. "Well, not really my house anymore. After this year I've gotta get my own place."

"That's my plan, too. Can't stand it anymore, man. You get along with your parents?"

"It's just my mom and stepdad."

"Oh--"

"My dad's not dead or anything."

"Oh."

"Just far away and shitty."

"Ha."

I put on a record to fill the air once we ran out of questions to ask one another. We unpacked to the sound of a dreamy melody, and I swear I heard him singing.

Chapter Two

Angela, still managing to remain my friend even after spending the summer together, walked with me to class whenever our schedules lined up.

"You have every month a new sworn boyfriend," she teased, misquoting her beloved Shakespeare. Ryan, too, was fond of the Bard, and the two of them had taken to running scenes together in the dorm. I tried to quell my jealousy, and Angela reminded me it was unfounded. "But I think this one might stick."

"I dunno," I said, adjusting the strap of my backpack on my ever-sloping shoulder. "I like him, obviously, but I don't even know if he's--"

"He is," she confirmed.

"He told you?"

"No, he cried while reading 'When Lilacs Last in The Dooryard Bloom'd' in class last week."

"Oh." I laughed at her attempt at proof. Angela was always funny, until she was sad, or cruel. Her jokes were her most obvious defense.

Once we parted ways, I attended my photojournalism class. It was effectively an hour and fifteen-minute slideshow, three days a week, where we tried to decide if the important historical moments captured on film were only important because they'd been seen and recorded. If anything, I said out loud with my hand raised, these photos were just documenting man's capability for violence and love, as those seemed to be the most common subjects.

It was bullshit, but my professor seemed impressed. By Junior year, everything you do is either bullshit or your opus. There is no... *in between*. By that time, you've learned how to navigate college work like channels in the ocean. It allowed me so much time for daydreaming.

It allowed me to stare out the classroom window, wondering what used to be in here. Wondering how many people suffered shocks or prodding to the brain to cure them of something that wasn't even wrong in the first place. I probably would have been there, strapped to a chair with electrodes stuck to my temples, getting the gay electrocuted out of me. I could have looked out this same window and seen my reflection just like I was right now. I counted myself lucky for living when I did, and where I did, even if I hated it. It could always be worse.

I thought about Ryan, about what it must have been like, if Angela was right, growing up gay in the south. I thought about his smile, and his arms, and how he let out the gentlest snores in his sleep. Despite their quiet nature, still they managed to wake me up in the middle of the night. I was always so vigilant. Ryan told me about how he sleeps like he's dead, because he'd lived next to so many animals for so long and had to get used to it. Even the rooster couldn't get him out of bed in the morning.

I thought about him in my bed. I thought about the two of us nestled impossibly close on the twin-sized mattress, its frame comically small against our long bodies. I thought about him, and thought and thought, ignoring the bloody images on the ancient projector, every face in the courtyard outside looking like his for one brief second. Wishful thinking, that I might get the chance to see him. Again, even though I saw him so often.

I thought about how, at night, he would take out his contacts. I thought about his thick-rimmed glasses and the stubble that grew on his upper lip by the end of every day.

When we were dismissed, and I struggled to get out of my chair, transfixed by my daydreams, I realized that Angela was right about at least one thing: this one was going to stick.

***

In the evening, when all the sky seemed to be dyed a deep orange, the three of us sat on my bed, books open but unread in our laps. It was the Friday sickness one feels when you know the weekend is just around the corner, so despite our exams and assignments and deadlines, we dallied instead. Ryan forewent his Wordsworth in favor of listening to me tell tales of the way this town used to be.

"So, they performed, like, lobotomies and shit?" he asked me, adjusting his position on the bed, leaning against the wall with his knees bent. The sparkle of curiosity in his eyes rendered me silent, but I nodded, trying not to swoon at the adorable way he pushed his glasses up his nose.

"They really try not to talk about it," Angela said. "Like we're supposed to just forget what this place was, as if it's not fucking bonkers."

"Is there anything left around from back then? EST machines or something?" Ryan asked, looking thrilled.

In truth, I had always wanted to find that evidence as well. To search all the places of the campus that we weren't allowed to go and do my job properly. Risking all the tetanus and jail time in the world, just to see something no one was supposed to see. But I was a coward through and through.

"I heard there's one building that's still got stuff in it," Angela said. I turned to look at her, not having heard of it myself. "In the basement."

"'Course it's in the god damn basement," Ryan laughed.

"You're so full of shit," I said to Angela, shoving her gently on the shoulder. She flipped me off, then slid off the bed.

"Am not," she insisted. "It's out by the old science building, the one that's been under construction since the dawn of time."

"Let's go see it," Ryan suggested, seeming all the more enticed by the idea. I worried, looking at him, that he was more enticed by Angela than by the mischief. But then he laid one hand on my knee and shook me just a little. My ears went hot, and my lips parted in a flutter. "Right, man? That'd be so cool."

Angela grinned, looking proud of herself, doing a little dance across the carpet. My eyes fixed on that strong hand as I considered the dangers. The worst-case scenario was hard to pin down. There was the possibility of disappointment, of course, that it would be completely empty. There was the risk of getting caught, which gave me a sort of nervous pit in my stomach. And, of course, something that felt like a very real threat then, as the sun continued to set and bathe the sky in darkness: that it would defy all reason and be full of ghosts, thereby forcing me to rethink my entire worldview while I died a horrible death.

He gave my knee the softest, encouraging squeeze.

"Yeah," I agreed, finally looking up, into his pleading eyes. I knew that, in reality, there were sounds other than the pounding of blood in my ears. I knew that there were distant, city-bound planes flying above, and that Angela was singing as she did her triumphant dance. But in that moment, the surrounding world seemed to fall away. I felt again as if I was doing something I oughtn't, enjoying even his most chaste touch as if it meant something deep and libidinal. It wasn't fair to him, was it; to relish in the slightest affection, to moon over a clueless man who just wanted to be my friend?

But he bit his lip as he grinned at me, and in a fugue state I felt myself place a hand on top of his.

"Okay," I said, redundant and transfixed. I knew it was stupid, to be floored by something so simple. To blush like a teenager and allow my mind to race and fill with thousands of possibilities as to why he was touching me. Isn't that what all the old magazines said? If a boy likes you, he'll go out of his way to make contact.

But Ryan wasn't some fifteen-year-old kid, and neither was I. At twenty-one, we didn't have to play by the same rules.

"Alright!" He retracted his hand and then clapped me fraternally on the back. As he slid off the bed and made his way over to Angela for a high-five, I felt my stomach sink.

Chapter Three

We agreed to wait until well after sundown, knowing that campus security liked to make their rounds right after it got dark. In the meantime, we walked up the road to the liquor store, ready to proudly flash our driver's licenses, wiping the smug look off the clerk's face.

But to our disappointment, as we purchased our six-dollar bottles of wine, he didn't even ask for ID.

In the gravel parking lot, we put the three bottles into my backpack, all the cheap glass padded by our sweatshirts, should the derelict house of horrors prove chilly.

"You got that, bud?" Ryan asked, probably noting how I grunted at the weight of it on my back. "We can take turns."

"It's alright," I told him, shifting the placement of the straps to make it more even. "I'm stronger than I look." I flexed my noodle arms then, and he laughed, melodiously.

"I bet you are," he said, once again leaving me reeling in a void of ambiguity. He walked on ahead, and as Angela set out behind him, she turned to me with her eyebrows raised in a way that could only be taken as suggestive.

I brought up the rear as we made our way down the road on its narrow, dangerous shoulder, our backs to the oncoming traffic. Each car that passed made me tense up, preparing to get hit. Eventually, I caught up with Ryan, having pathetically quickened my pace for that very goal.

"You okay?" he asked me, watching as I nervously inched away from the edge of the road.

"Just don't wanna get hit," I said with a shrug. By then he'd become accustomed to only some of my little anxieties and neuroses. It seemed I revealed a new one to him every day, and I was waiting for which one would be the tipping point. Which little insecurity would finally get him to roll his eyes or scoff?

"Switch with me," he said, grabbing my arm, pulling me gently past him, so that he was the one closest to the road instead. "That feel better?"

He was so kind, I realized. Any friend I'd had before might have feigned a shove toward the road, might have chided me for being too skittish and paranoid.

"...thank you," I said finally, looking down to my shoes, kicking at the gravel and mud. He let his hand fall down my arm, briefly brushing my fingers, hesitating a moment as if to grab my hand.

"Not a problem," he assured me, and then he went on walking. "You sure you're gonna be okay sneakin' into this place?"

"I'm more afraid of cars than of ghosts, because cars actually exist," I said.

"You really don't believe in ghosts?" he asked me, genuine and curious. I walked alongside on the uneven ground and nodded. "Never seen one?"

"No," I told him. "Do you believe in them?"

He shrugged.

"Ain't ready to rule it out, is all."

Ryan, I'd learned, was a man of faith. Not to any evangelical, preachy extent, but enough to actually believe in something, and remain open-minded about the ways of the universe. I blamed it on his upbringing. Blamed, as if it had to be a bad thing. He had proven it wasn't. I didn't believe in anything, myself. I admired that he hadn't lost that capacity, while I couldn't even fathom a god.

Once we reached the old building, the campus was utterly dark. It was an old section, last used before the advent of motion-sensing lights. Before we made our attempt to break in, we opened the first bottle of wine. Angela took the first gulp, then Ryan, and then me, and I tried not to get too hung up on the idea that his lips had touched it. Tried, but failed, and found myself trying to taste him there. His soft, never-chapped lips.

Even with just an ounce or two of booze in me, I managed to become so capable of swooning. But I held fast to trying to appear as if I wasn't infatuated.

Angela, ever-mysterious in her resourcefulness, pulled some bobby pins from her pocket and inspected the rusty padlock on the old door.

"Luc, you keep watch," she commanded in a furtive whisper, and she knelt before the door, whipping her yarn braids over her shoulders, sticking her tongue out as if that might help her focus. "Ryan, gimme some light."

"Yes ma'am," he said with a chuckle, elbowing me gently in the arm as he pulled out his phone to shine the light. I grinned stupidly, overwhelmed by his charm, as one always gets during a *newish* crush. Everything they say and everything they do is always funnier, braver, more brilliant. You look at them with the fabled rose-colored glasses, and you swear that they will still be just as divine when you take them off.

I wasn't worried so much about him. Ryan, I felt, could still be perfect even as time passed. I was more worried that, even if he should like me now, it wouldn't last. That there would eventually be something about me that would piss him off, and it would be the last straw. That always seemed to be the way it happened with me. I would meet some guy, and he would find my scrawny shape amusing. He would see my anxiety as something he could fix, and when he failed to do so, I would become too frustrating and no longer a worthwhile project.

I lit a cigarette. I was down to two a day.

I scanned the horizon for anyone who might see us. It was dead out there, everyone still pregaming in their dorms before their Friday really began.

I heard a satisfied grunt from Angela, and then the sound of the padlock falling to the ground.

"Phew…" She grabbed for the open bottle of wine and drank some more, refreshing herself after her hard work.

"Incredible," Ryan said.

"Sometimes I think you're in the wrong major, Angela," I said.

"Well, they don't offer degrees in being a thief," she told us.

"They do," Ryan said. "It's called being a business major."

Our laughter echoed into the empty building as Angela pushed open the heavy door. It immediately looked like a nightmare, even just from what we could see. The door opened into a long, tiled hallway, the ceiling fit with falling fluorescent lights. We all shined our lights down the hall, looking at the decay, the black mold and the scurrying rats.

"Nasty," Angela said. "Come on."

I hesitated at the threshold. I wondered if that was how kids felt, back before this place got cleaned up. I would have been one of the chickens, I thought. I would never prove myself. And I didn't even believe in ghosts.

"S'alright, bud," Ryan said, reaching for my hand to pull me into the dark. Angela was already trudging on ahead. "No ghosts, remember?"

I felt like a child, needing to be encouraged so gently. Or at least, that is how I imagined it was like to feel like a child that someone gave a shit about. Maybe every failed relationship was my fault, actually. I always needed someone else to be the grownup.

But there I was, six-foot-one, with a backpack full of alcohol, and the warm palm of another man pressed to mine. I ignored how few miles there were then, between me and my childhood home. I curled my fingers around his hand and stepped into the abyss.

Our footsteps echoed as we walked, as if the building seemed to grow impossible larger around us. We kept our lights ever-swinging, not wanting to miss an inch of scenery, not wanting to pass the basement door that would either thrill or disappoint us.

Eventually, we came to the obvious threshold: large, army-green double doors with a push bar. Angela grinned, and then lifted her phone.

"And we're rolling. Coming to you live from the Northeast State, our ace reporter Lucas Lopes is on the scene," she said, taking on the stale enthusiasm of an anchorwoman.

"Come on..." I put my hand up in front of her phone. "You're practically begging for this to turn into a horror movie," I said.

"Don't be shy, Lucas," she said, pouting, but lowering the camera nonetheless.

"You ask a lot of me."

"Y'all are just wasting time because you're scared to go down there," Ryan said, gently admonishing us. "Let's open this thing."

He pushed his hands into the bar, and it gave with a loud creak. He managed to get one of the double doors open, and he held it for me and Angela as we entered the basement. As I passed him, I gave him an appreciative smile. His green eyes seemed to glow in the dark. As he let the door shut behind him, he placed a guiding hand on my shoulder from behind me.

Hours ago, I might have decided it was one of those teenage excuses for touch. But now I just felt like he thought I was a coward. And as much as I knew I ought to prove him wrong, the heavy feeling of his hand on my back was just too welcome for me to shrug him away.

We walked down the wooden stairs in a single-file line, each holding onto the hem of the shirt of the person in front of us. I was in the middle, and I could feel Ryan there, his knuckles against the small of my back, nothing but the fabric of my t-shirt between his skin and the elastic band of my underwear. It was nothing new, as he'd seen me in nothing but that, more than once. I'd seen him, too, fresh from the shower, his tight, black, short-legged boxer briefs clinging to his strong body as if made for him and him alone. And me, gangly in my boxers.

But now, fully-clothed, it was somehow more nerve-wracking to be near him. I blamed it on the horrors that laid below.

Once we reached the bottom of the stairs, we saw what we were not supposed to see. Finally, I could project that voyeuristic feeling onto something that didn't make me giddy, but just made me uncomfortable.

There was a table with folded white hospital gowns, a collection of leather straps and straightjackets in a massive laundry bin, and a few leather gurneys strewn about.

"Huh..." Ryan mused, walking in further. "'Nothin' beside remains,' I guess."

"This is it?" Angela asked, venomous and tipsy. She approached me to unzip my backpack and take out the second bottle of wine. "I was hoping to see some really fucked up shit."

We sat at the bottom of the stairs for an hour or so, passing the wine to one another, positing where there might be more little enclaves of evidence of this place's past. Maybe they burned everything. Maybe we were just patients having a group hallucination, and this wasn't a school at all. That was my favorite theory.

Ryan and I were beside one another as we all talked, and I found he kept sliding his hand farther along the wooden step, farther behind my back. In my intoxication, I allowed myself to lean back into his arm.

Angela heaved a sigh. She always reached that point in the evening when she could no longer smile, could no longer keep up with herself. She left with a vague goodbye.

"She alright?" Ryan asked me, his lips hovering over the mouth of the third bottle.

"She just gets sad," I told him. "She says she...builds up these nights in her head, and even if she has fun, it feels empty." Like a birthday, the older you got.

"Yeah..." He sounded like he had a deep understanding of the plight. In the dark, lit by nothing but our phones, I could see his eyes cast down at the concrete floor. "Nothin's ever as good as we want it to be." He took a sip. "Ugh-- this, for example."

I laughed as he passed me the unwanted bottle, and despite his warning, I took a generous gulp. Anything to get rid of the last bit of nerves I still had. It was all so quickly evaporating. I felt his eyes on me as I swallowed, and I made slow work of tilting the bottle back down, of removing my lips from the glass mouth. I watched his eyes travel my face, watched his playful smile fade into something a bit more somber. Something I could mold into whatever I wanted it to be. I pretended that he was looking at me with desire. I pretended we were somewhere very far away, and that he could love me.

His thumb ran up and down my lower back where he was propped up by his hand. Everything was so quiet.

But then, the loudest of sounds. The door to the building swung open, and light suddenly leaked in from underneath the basement door.

"Shit," I said, gathering up the wine and my backpack. There came some vague, angry, booming voice from the other side of the door.

"We gotta hide," Ryan said, grabbing my wrist, taking me swiftly to some dark corner of the basement.

My back against the wall, he pressed a finger to my lips. I nodded slowly, acutely aware of how my lips were brushing against his skin.

It was as unavoidable as imagining yourself getting hit by a car when you're walking along a busy road. A man presses his fingers to your mouth, and you can't help but imagine them going in deep.

The security officer was descending the stairs. We stood stock-still and close, squished into the corner together. I realized then that I was curling my fingers into the fabric of his shirt, and that our bodies were flush.

I wanted him, then. And I imagined that he wanted me, too. I felt ready to risk getting caught, just to share one kiss in a musty basement, surrounded by the relics of worse days.

The guard made a cursory sweep of the basement with his flashlight, missing us just barely. In our triumph, we grinned at one another, fighting victorious laughter, wrinkling our noses at the thrill of having gotten away with it. Once we heard the basement door close again, we allowed ourselves to exhale.

We waited to hear the front door open and close one last time, and then ascended the stairs to make our quick escape. We ran, stealthy as we could, hand-in-hand, to the door, and stood close to peer through the porthole windows and make sure the coast was clear.

We bolted back to the tower in a fit of childish giggling. That night, dizzy and exhausted from the long evening, too sheepish to mention what had happened, we fell asleep in separate beds.

Chapter Four

The school paper was finally up and running again by late September. I was tasked with reporting on political events on campus, so when I wasn't studying or hanging out with Ryan and Angela, I was attending rallies and protests. Of course, the only story in the paper that anyone cared about was a security guard's account of a strange encounter he had in the old science building.

"We're famous," Ryan said. I took a moment to appreciate that 'we.' "Guess we ain't going back there any time soon."

"I'm okay with that," I admitted.

We were enjoying the last bastions of nice autumn weather, sitting on the quad with our textbooks between us. Ryan looked like the sort of man who was meant to exist in the fall. How his collarbone peaked out from his wool sweaters, the slight glimpse of his knee-high socks beneath the cuff of his jeans. I tried to imagine him in winter, spring, summer. In every season he made me sweat, no matter the weather.

Things had changed since that night. It was as if some dam had been broken between us, and things had become so much more tender, domestic. When I made coffee in the morning, I would wake him up with the smell and the news that I'd already put in just the right amount of milk. At night, we would stay up too late, just talking until we were too tired to open our mouths.

He became comfortable enough to share his poems with me. I, though a poor judge, thought they were beautiful, but that wasn't what I said out loud.

"That's awesome," I said, holding onto the print-out of something he'd called a sestina.

"It's like a puzzle," he told me. "You gotta find where the words fit, and when you get it right, it makes the whole picture."

I thought about how we fit together. I thought about how I was certain that, if I let myself be that stupid, there would come a time when I could no longer tell where I ended and he began.

The intimacies were subtle at first. That reassuring hand on my shoulder while I sat at my desk, writing an article, trying my best to be objective. Me, holding the door for him, my elbow so knobby on my outstretched arm. And still we existed as any roommates might, not minding the near-nudity, minding our own business and vacating the room when one of us needed to get off. And I hated myself, alone in there, unable to help but think about him, no matter what lewd images were actually in front of me. It was always him. I couldn't stop the fantasy.

The lust was so constant that, when it finally did happen, I was certain for a while afterwards that it had been a dream.

There seemed to be no clear impetus for it. It was, I realize now, inevitable. From the moment he stepped off that train and I felt within me that happy dread, there was nowhere else he could end up but inside of me, and inside of my heart.

He came back from class one evening when I was just getting undressed from the day. I stood there, before the mirror, inspecting the bones of my own body and finding them wanting. My hair, ever a mess, was pushed behind my ears, and the bags beneath my eyes I'd had since birth seemed to be twofold heavy from stress.

As the door opened, I made no attempt to cover myself. It was as if I wanted him to see my shame, and the reason for it, even though he'd seen it before. But when he saw me, the look on his face seemed full of reverence. He smiled, his eyes half-lidded and softly gazing, and dropped his bag on the floor as he approached me. I turned to him expectantly, trying desperately to glean the meaning from his movements. Hoping he was coming toward me with the same hunger I'd been trying to hide since late August.

Both of us nervous and unsure, we faced each other. Ryan ran his hands down my arms, and I felt as if he could utterly snap me in two, if he wanted. I would let him. I was his.

"You really gotta stop being so down on yourself, bud," he told me then, as if between us we had developed some telepathy. With one of his strong fingers, he lifted my chin to look me directly in the eyes. He seemed to drink me in, then, staring at me in a way I'd seen before, but could never name. I gave it many excuses, the staring. That he was spacing out, that I had something in my teeth. But I realized then that it had been nothing but a mirror.

He laid a palm flat on my sternum, and I swore I could feel his pulse, so strong from his wrist, racing away at a rate unsustainable. My heart, against his hand, beat just as fast.

"I mean, I think you're..." He gulped. "You know..."

Seeing him falter was a revelation. The rose-colored glasses were torn from the bridge of my nose, and I saw him not as the unflappable Southern charmer I'd thought he was when we met, but as a real, whole, terrified person. The look in his eyes was familiar to me, that fear. I, of course, had experienced it years before him. The fear you feel when you realize you want something that, according to others, you shouldn't.

"God damn, bud, I dunno…" He bit his lip and ran that hand down my chest, my stomach. I felt, in the light of his subtle worship, very brave.

"Say it," I said, gently begging. I stepped closer, daring to lift my hands to surround his cheeks. They felt hot to the point of burning. I pleaded with him to say it, to say anything, to cut the heavy fog that seemed to have permeated through the windows, bringing the vast and open sky into our room.

He said nothing. He slid his arms around my waist and kissed me. Nervous, at first, a single peck on my parted lips. Clumsy, and with poor aim. And then another, and another, as if chipping away at his fear. It sent through me a shiver that radiated to my every limb. I curled my toes, and with a heavy exhale, I helped him get past the sheer terror of the risky feat of kissing your roommate.

I felt him open his jaw, felt him sink into me, no longer afraid, knowing then that this was what I wanted, what he wanted. I tossed my arms over his shoulders and bent them around the back of his neck, tilting my hips into his, giving myself up. When I felt his tongue slide along my lower lip, I could not help the happy groan that left me.

The sound seemed to thrill him, and he curled his fingers into my naked back, pulling me toward him, bidding me to walk until he was against the wall.

I had never before experienced him this way: subject to anything, anyone, and miraculously, it was me. In his apparent adoration of me, I saw him made weak for the very first time. I slid my hands back over his neck, feeling the smooth plane of his skin, running my thumb over the shivering apple of his throat.

He bravely pushed his tongue past my teeth. The hot, wet sensation elicited from me another warm gasp, and his breathing seemed to grow heavier and more labored. With our hips pressed together, I began to feel him growing stiff against me. I too, began to give myself over to the pulsing feeling, every drop of blood my wanting body could spare, rushing between my legs, leaving my head all dizzy and light from his affections, from my own excitement.

He seemed to hold me so sweetly. As he slid his hands back up my chest, I felt the rough, workman's callouses of his fingers, in direct contrast to my own untrained skin. Just then, as his hands reached the sides of my neck, he pulled away from the long, wet kiss, and licked away the string of saliva we'd left between us. He stared me down, looking more serious than I'd ever seen him.

Overwhelmed with adoration, my hands seemed controlled as if by some invisible tether, drawn to press my palm against the struggling fly of his jeans. At the first touch, he leaned his head back against the wall with a subtle thump and grinned as if in rapture. He looked almost relieved, as if these past few months had, in his mind as well, been leading to this. Like maybe his daydreams and his sleeping were also filled with me, and maybe I was better than his imagination.

I had to prove that to him, then. I used both hands to unbutton his jeans, and he looked down as if in disbelief at my eagerness. Once his zipper was down, I slipped my hand beneath the waistband of his underwear, and finally, I felt it. Almost coyly at first, hiding my face in his neck to kiss, I ghosted my fingers over the tip. He shuddered, curling his fingers into my shoulders yet again, holding me there so desperately, as if terrified I might stop touching him.

Elated by the feeling of his taut skin, I surrounded his cock-- and God, it seemed just the perfect size-- with my fingers. I gripped him, firm but tender, running one thumb up and down the length of him, giving him just a taste.

A taste. My throat felt empty.

He guided me by the jaw, away from my hiding place, to kiss him again as I began to jerk him off. Not with the same hastiness I'd done with myself. I treated him as one might handle something precious. Pumping away so caringly, ecstatic at the feeling of his warm skin and the rock-hard lust.

I had to see it. I had to taste it.

Pulling out of the kiss with another moan, I looked down between us, saw him fully erect there, his skin awash with the soft red glow of want. As he removed his shirt, pulling it clumsily over his head, I dropped to my knees.

At first, I just admired it. Held it in my hand like a prize, and let the tip brush against my flushed cheek, my tongue shyly slipping from the corner of my mouth to drag it along. I felt as if I was standing on the edge of a welcoming void. That, once I did this, there would be no turning back. It was so god damn perfect. I measured it with my eyes, too flustered and dizzy for the math of it, and decided that it might be the dreamiest cock I'd ever seen.

And before I could take him fully into my mouth, I looked up. He had a hand pressed to his forehead, the other running through his now-messy hair, utterly disheveled and radiating awe. I felt, for the first time, not so ugly in comparison. No one looks at someone that way, no one squirms like that, if the person kneeling before their dick isn't beautiful to them.

I kissed the tip, first. He twitched, and I grinned, parting my lips just enough to take it in, tightening them just-so around the entire head. My mouth wet, I allowed my hungry tongue to circle him, slowly taking more and more of him past my lips, milking my throat for saliva, coating him thickly, parting my jaw farther than it ought to go.

I felt hands in my hair. He tucked some stray strands behind my ear then. So enamored of his sweet touch, I could no longer wait. I gripped gently onto his hips and descended on him in full. I felt him in the back of my mouth, that most satisfying, full sensation, and I could not help but smile around him, my brow stitching into an overjoyed curve, just so happy to be there, so happy to taste him.

I pulled down his jeans all the way, just wanting more of him, however much of him I could get. With one hand, I reached beneath his dick to hold his balls. Even his strong and sturdy legs seemed to shake, and his fingers ran through the knots of my hair, the slight stinging of my scalp making me happily hum as I surrounded him.

"Lucas..." he said, if only to hear my name in a new light. One's name takes on a new sound, once you've been down their throat. It sounded more like a prayer, and not a way to get my attention. He already had it. All of it, and in my glee at that moment, I thought maybe he might have it forever.

As I bobbed my head, changing the shape of my mouth to fit whichever part of him I passed over, I sucked, hard, humming happily all the while to show him how I loved the taste, how I felt the strength of his dick pushing past where my gag reflex ought to kick in. For him, I ignored the involuntary feeling. I'd always been good at sucking dick, but in blowing him I felt I had advanced to some new level of skill, where I could choke on him and never feel sick.

"Holy shit--" he gasped. I felt him begin to tilt his hips into me, and I moved along with his rhythm, enjoying the feeling of his strong hands surrounding the back of my head, but never pulling or pushing too hard. We worked together that way, and I felt him grow impossibly in my mouth, tasted the first few leaking drops of cum and heard the weak, whining noises from his throat that told me he was almost finished. I tried not to be too proud of myself but could barely help it. With a few final, grunting thrusts, I felt him explode, and then he held still, as if waiting for me to pull away and be unwilling to swallow. But I kept him in my mouth, one hand still on his balls, the other wrapping around the base of his dick as he came. I waited until the final joyful spasms, waited for him to give me everything he had, and then tilted my head back to release him back into the cool air of the room.

I looked into his eyes as I gulped it down. His gaze was glossed over, his skin flushed from his chest up, his knees threatening to knock together.

I sealed it with a kiss, and he laughed as he shook, still so sensitive from orgasm.

He exhaled, and dropped to his knees as well, to meet me. His breathing still heavy, he kissed my cheek, and then the other, covering me in a flurry of appreciative kisses. Speechless, but still wanting somehow to thank me.

For the first time, then, he hugged me. Arms wrapped tight around my slender shoulders, resting his nose in the curve of my neck. And though I was still achingly hard, I felt no immediate need to come. I simply basked in the joy of being impressive, the joy of having gotten my fill. Eventually, we dressed. We headed chastely to the dining hall, sharing a new bashfulness between us, but still not daring to carry our intimacy into public.

Chapter Five

Things continued on similarly for the rest of the semester. We would attend class, go about our days as if nothing at all had changed, and then in the evenings, rush back to our dorm and into bed. We always stopped just short of actually fucking, as Ryan still seemed kind of wary of embracing what I could only assume was a newly-discovered part of himself. I wasn't brave enough to ask, or to beg for him to tell me he cared for me, maybe even could love me.

All I wanted to do was blow him. He, in his kindness and beauty, had hypnotized me into adoring his cock as if it were made of something divine. All I wanted to do was be near him, but I couldn't get myself to ask if he felt just as devoted.

I pretended that he was. I collected the evidence. How he would sometimes fall asleep on my bed, how he would pet my hair after I made him come. He even touched me, nervously, laying there with his head resting on my chest, looking down as he stroked my cock.

When December arrived, the sadness settled in with the cold. We would soon be leaving for nearly a month on winter break, going back to our respective homes. Or, in my case, Angela's home. I'd been invited to stay in the guest room at my mother's house, but the thought of spending an entire freezing cold month in the place that contained the memories of some of my worst times was fairly unappealing.

After our last finals that semester, we were packing up what we would need for break, deciding what could be left behind until we came back. In my usual fashion, I stuffed whatever clothes I felt like I would wear into a suitcase, while Ryan folded his neatly into categories.

"You really not gonna see your folks, bud?" he asked me, hoisting himself up onto my mattress as I packed, still using that simple, friendly nickname as if it had become something much more tender. "Like, at all?"

I shook my head.

"We don't exactly get along," I told him. I'd given him the skeleton of the story in a few vague installments. But just then, he had such a look of sympathy on his face I couldn't help but explain. I sat beside him, my head on his shoulder. I told him about my stepfather, how he thought I was some sort of deviant, how my mother tended to mold herself into whatever he wanted her to be. How I'd always been a lonely kid, voluntarily. Anxious all the time, sometimes brooding and inconsolable. I was a frustrating child. Being gay was just the final reason they needed to justify why they didn't want me. Ryan put an arm around my shoulder.

"That's shitty," he said, and he kissed the top of my head. I decided then that he loved me, and I didn't have to plead with him to say it out loud.

We promised to text. It was so unlike our generation to actually make a phone call unless you were about to die and wanted to confess something you'd been keeping inside for years, so I didn't try to bargain for more.

He kissed me goodbye. His train was leaving soon. Down to Grand Central, then Penn Station to get on an impossibly long bus ride back to Charleston. His father's obsession with work ethic kept him from having the luxury of plane tickets.

Again, like a voyeur, I watched him walk onto the train platform from the window where first I saw him, and I lit a cigarette. I was down to one a day, and I always saved it for the hardest moments.

As the door slid shut, as the train jolted into motion, I mumbled to no one that I would miss him.

Angela lived in a raised ranch farther upstate on the outskirts of Utica. Utica always seemed to me like a place just pretending to be a city, a hodge-podge of ugly buildings where it seemed to always be raining. She hated it, too, but her family was just as broke as mine, so they had no choice but to stay.

I was greeted by a tight hug from Angela's mother, and then she showed me to the couch in the basement as if I had never been there before. She was a gracious host, very obviously missing her only child, thrilled to have extra one to dote on when she came home.

"So, Lucas," her father asked in his booming voice over that first dinner. "How's your love life?" He always asked that and sounded as though he felt obligated to make the extra effort to show that he didn't disapprove of what he still, in his advanced age, called my 'lifestyle.'

"He's got a hot new boyfriend," Angela interjected, chewing on her steak with a wide, proud grin on her face.

"Angela Marie, keep your mouth closed when you chew," her mother said. "Is that true, Lucas? You're seeing someone?" I shrugged, still feeling as though I didn't have permission to call him my boyfriend. Boyfriends went out together holding hands, didn't they? They called home to gush about each other, and they told all their friends.

"Kinda," I admitted. "We're not really putting a label on it or anything."

"That, my boy, is some bullshit," Angela's father said, pointing his fork at me. "You either like someone enough to be with them, or you don't. Back in our day we didn't fuck around with 'not putting a label on it.'"

"George, you always cuss after a glass of wine," Angela's mother scolded, though she was smiling adoringly at him.

"Back in our day you just dated each other and no one had to make a big deal about hiding their feelings and all that shit," he went on. "'A label.'" He scoffed. "Angela, don't tell me you ever let some guy spend all his time with you and refuse to call you his girlfriend."

"Dad." Her eyes were wide and she slumped in her chair a little bit, desperate for him to drop the subject.

Together, the three of them cut the tension with happy laughter. I joined in, and the rest of the dinner conversation was muted by the echoing of Angela's father's advice in my head.

That first night when I went to lay down on the couch, I checked my phone, finding a few texts from Ryan, and a paragraph-long guilt trip from my mother. I ignored the latter and opened the texts from Ryan. One of them was a picture of the Charleston skyline at sunset. Another was asking if I made it to Angela's safely, and it warmed my heart. The third was an absolutely intoxicating picture of his erect penis, held gently between his fingers. I nearly spat, blinking in surprise, pressing a hand to my chest as if so happily scandalized. I licked my lips.

I couldn't care, in that moment, what our label would end up being. I was too distraught that I was about to spend a whole month only being able to look at him and not touch. But I texted him back with a photo of my own, and the sweetest words I could think to say without being too needy.

"I'm gonna miss you."

I got myself off beneath the itchy blanket on the couch, eyes closed, only opening to catch a fluttering glance at that photo, and to see if I'd received anything back. I fell asleep right after, dick in my hand, my phone silent and still.

In the bleary morning I was awoken by the smell of the too-strong coffee Angela's father makes. I grabbed my phone immediately and rubbed my eyes to prepare for the inevitable disappointment. But there was a text from Ryan, as well as a reminder that I'd yet to read my mother's guilt trip. I ignored it again in favor of seeing whatever Ryan had said in response to my pathetic attempt at acting like someone he could call his boyfriend.

"I already miss you," he'd written. I grinned and held my phone to my chest, taking in a deep breath of the coffee-filled air. It would be strong, and I couldn't wait to feel fully awake. I felt the rare desire to be alert and alive.

Chapter Six

My heart had been racing for the entire long drive down from Utica. I felt all at once hot and cold, the nervous feeling climbing my spine and filling my entire dizzy head. Angela's attempts at calming me down were fruitless, but I tried to still appreciate them. Seeing him again, after all this time…'All this time,' as if a month isn't so small in the grand scheme of things.

"Don't throw up," she told me. "My dad'll kill you if you mess up the car seats."

I nodded and bent down, putting my head between my knees. It wasn't as though I hadn't spoken to him at all. It wasn't as if I hadn't heard his voice. We had spoken on the phone, a feat all its own, considering our shared aversion to it. But after a week of nothing but texting, we were finally ready to admit that we had missed the sound of one another.

I still couldn't tell him, though, that I was certain I loved him. Or, at the very least, that I was barreling toward it. He told me about his winter farm work, splitting wood with an axe. I imagined his strong arms reaching toward the sky, and then coming down in one swift motion, tearing through the logs as if they were made of butter. We exchanged dirty pictures, spoke into the wee hours of the morning, until we fell asleep with our phones beneath our heads like pillows.

So, I couldn't justify the abject terror I felt on that car ride, the absolute doom I felt was waiting for me on campus.

I carried my bags with shaking elbows, bidding Angela's family goodbye, and rode the elevator up to the eleventh floor. It stopped, of course, at every floor, students filing in and out, crowding the tiny car, making everything seem so much worse, making the journey back to him feel so much longer.

By the time the elevator got to the eleventh floor, I was alone within the car. I winced at the electronic bell that preceded the opening of the doors, and I gulped down whatever nervous whining I felt I might produce against my own will.

The hallway stretched out just like the one in the abandoned science building, but the fear I had felt then was nothing compared to this. When I finally got to our door, I could hear familiar music creeping out from under it. I recognized it as the record we'd listened to when he'd moved in. I blushed at the gesture, knowing Ryan to live poetically, even when he wasn't writing. I wondered how long he'd been planning that little detail, if he'd have known how much it would mean to me.

I opened the door, trying to trick myself into looking normal, and not like I was vibrating with nerves and a months-long lust. Just then, at the cathartic crescendo of the song, Ryan came to me with his arms outstretched, and I dropped my bags to the ground. He embraced me, swaying, and I swore I could feel him smiling as our cheeks pressed together. We breathed there for a moment, our chests rising and falling together. The nausea seemed to dissolve from me the longer he held me in his arms.

Eventually, when our song ended, he retreated just enough to look at me. I knew my eyes were glassy, and though I was embarrassed at being so emotional, he didn't appear to mind.

We talked extraordinarily little. We fell onto his bed and made up for every lost moment, and we touched each other with such rapture it all felt brand new. I begged to suck him off.

"As long as, uh…" He scratched the back of his head. "I wanna do you, too."

Apparently, in his time away from me, he'd grown a little braver, a little more comfortable. I nodded, feverish to a shameful degree, and then began my familiar descent down his body.

When it was my turn, he laid me down on the too-small bed and palmed at the nearly painful erection I had gotten, so overwhelmingly turned on from finally having him back in my mouth where he belonged. He took me in with a smile, though I could read his uncertainty clear as day. Thus, I tried to encourage him as much as I could without being patronizing. But eventually, I lost myself to the pleasure, and laid still, my head propped up on his pillow, watching him love me. It had to be that, right? It was just too sweet, the way he handled me.

And then, both spent and our lips gone slack from all that work, we laid side-by-side in a pile of arms and legs, talking quietly.

It began again, just as it had in December. That phase where you cannot keep your hands off one another. When you go crazy from not sleeping, and when everything you eat is bad for you, because that's all that's available at two in the morning. And maybe you put on a little weight, and maybe your grades slip, but you get by. Everything around you becomes secondary, and you have to rush through it blindly, just to get back home and touch and taste.

That thing I'd warned myself against was happening, and it was out of my control. Whenever he wasn't near me, it felt as though I was missing a part of my body. A part of our puzzle.

Angela teased me often about it but admitted that she also just wanted something like that. Even if it wasn't love. She wanted someone to look at her the way Ryan and I looked at each other. Like we could eat one another alive.

By March, we were holding hands in public. We were going out to restaurants and bars and showing up to parties with one another. We had become a unit. But still, when I was introduced, I was just Lucas. Not my boyfriend Lucas. It was as if the word tasted bad in his mouth, and I followed suit, still not wanting to overstep.

Angela echoed her father on that predicament.

"What is wrong with you men?" she asked me one evening as we shared mozzarella sticks in the dining hall. "Just be like: 'I love you, let's keep doing the same shit we've already been doing.'"

"I don't want to change things," I told her, my prepared excuse. "What we've got going on is good, okay?"

She stuck out her tongue. I threw a balled-up napkin her way.

We went outside. I lit a cigarette. Still clinging to one a day but trying not to use it as a crutch.

By May I had quit entirely. I worried, out loud, as Ryan and I lay naked together in the morning, that I had simply replaced one addiction with another. He shook his head.

"Just be proud of yourself, bud," he insisted. I agreed silently, and then buried my head in his welcoming chest. He surrounded me with his arms. "I was thinkin'..."

I gulped. That kind of preamble could lead to something devastating.

"Yeah?" I asked, muffled by his skin.

"What are you doing for summer?" he asked me. I shrugged in his arms. I felt his lips against the top of my head. "You could...I dunno, come to the farm."

I lifted my head, looking at him with wide and curious eyes.

"Yeah?" That was all I could manage.

"I know you don't wanna see your mom. N' you always stay with Angela. I thought, maybe..." He shrugged as well. I saw then, what Angela had been complaining about regarding us men.

"I'd like that," I told him, laying my head back down on the pillow. Grinning, he kissed me, once or twice, the kind where you think the first one will be enough, but it never really is, so you keep going back for more.

"Just one thing," he went on, turning to lay on his back again. He folded his arms behind his head. "We can't exactly uh...tell my dad about this."

And there was the devastation, though mild compared to what it could have been.

"That's fine. As long as..." I hesitated. "As long as there's something there to keep secret..."

He was quiet for a moment.

"Of course there is."

Chapter Seven

From the train and the bus, I could watch the landscape change. The farther down the Atlantic coast we clambered, the thicker the early summer air seemed to be. Even in the safe embrace of the air conditioning, I could feel how the outside sweltered. Ryan, ever a sweetheart, had given me the window seat for the entire trip so that I might press my forehead against the glass, marveling at the gradual change of the scenery.

By the time we crossed the border into South Carolina, everything seemed to flatten and dry.

"You gotta be careful of red ants," he warned me as I stared at the sand along the side of the road, how it seemed to glow. "Which sucks, because this is barefoot weather."

I turned to him, inquisitive.

"Barefoot weather?"

"Yeah, when you don't wanna wear shoes, because the grass is so refreshing, and you kinda feel like a cave person."

I couldn't imagine communing with the earth so freely, so brazenly exposing my skin to dirt and bugs. But, as he did everywhere, Ryan seemed like he could belong barefoot in the South Carolinian terrain, red ants be damned. For the remainder of the trip, we sat with our heads leaning together and our hands clasped between the seats, saying a silent goodbye to our presumed last chance for visible intimacy.

But Ryan cut through the reticence.

"Gonna be hard," he said with a sigh.

"Hm?" I felt sleepy from the steady rocking off the coach bus.

"Bein' around you. Not acting like...you know."

"Yeah--" I interrupted myself with a yawn.

"Maybe we can sneak away sometimes," he suggested.

The mischief of it thrilled me. Perhaps our little adventure in the basement of that old building had made me the kind of person who takes risks.

Or, what's more likely, I was willing to take a risk if it meant getting more of his absolving love.

I fell asleep and was awoken by the screeching stop of the bus. Ryan shook me awake, and kissed my temple with his eyes open, focusing on the bus station outside, careful not to do it in front of his father's assistant, who he'd told me about. He was Mr. Meade's right-hand man and who I assumed was also his resident narc. Though, despite his unwavering loyalty, Carlos was at least an allegedly kind man.

We held hands until the very last second of privacy, when we began to descend the stairs that led us off the bus. I was immediately suffocated by the heat. The air down there just smelled different, tastes different. Not necessarily cleaner, but with a sort of untouched purity I guessed was the source of the mythical Southern laid-back attitude.

But all bus stations are exactly alike, and this one was not spared the chaos of shuffling to one's respective taxi, et cetera. Carlos, a stout man wearing an honest-to-God bolo tie, waved us down from beneath the awning, and Ryan waved excitedly at him, then nodded for me to follow as fast as I could. I navigated the crowd with a relative ease but found myself out of breath by the time we caught up to Carlos. He clapped Ryan on the back and reached to take his larger suitcase.

I shook his hand. He had a studious gaze, which unnerved me. It seemed like he was too perceptive for a normal person, that his mind was trained like a detective's. I supposed I ought to feel some kinship, as a budding journalist, because of his apparent penchant for finding the truth. After a few seconds of discerning staring, he smiled at me, and began to lead us to his car.

This seemed to me like pickup truck country. Every engine around us was as loud as the bus, and the air, in its less-pure pockets, smelled of gasoline. But Carlos's Cadillac shone in the sun like a beacon of wealth. Mr. Meade must pay his staff pretty well, I thought. I wondered, then, why Ryan wasn't offered, as he'd put it, 'jack shit' for all his hard work. The car was painted a deep burgundy, and the interior was all made of yellow-brown leather that stuck to my skin when we sat down in the back seat. Carlos blasted the ice-cold air conditioning and put on the classic rock station, asking vague questions about how school is, how we met, on and on.

I let the two of them catch up, opting instead to continue my routine of leaning my head against the window to study my surroundings. All that orange sand, all those novelty adobe buildings and old colonials. I knew there had to be a reason why Ryan was desperate to leave, as everyone is always desperate to leave the place where they grew up. But Charleston was beautiful. It was nothing like the impossibly dull swamp where I grew up, where we went to school, where I had long felt I was doomed to die, as well. I allowed my fantasy to grow so much more innocent, then. I thought about leaving Wingdale after college, coming down to Charleston and buying a wide, white house with a wrap-around porch and a big backyard. Any dream would do, living where I did. Charleston. New York. The West coast. My imagination stretched toward anywhere that was different from what I'd known.

And I hoped that Ryan might be there too, wherever I ended up. I tried not to bet on it. But it was difficult, when I turned my head to look at him again, and I saw his sweet, enthusiastic grin as he told Carlos stories from our time at school. I guessed he had already shared the basement incident, save for a few details, over winter break. I imagined watching that smile earn its wrinkles, but never lose its brightness.

The private drive to the Meade Family Farm was marked with a hand-carved wooden sign. The entrance was cut into a field of high grass and seemed to stretch back into infinity with its sand, well-worn tire tracks.

"Hope you're ready to work, Lucas," Carlos said to me, looking in the rearview mirror. Ryan had explained to me that staying with him that summer did mean I'd have to partake in some hard labor, and I had agreed. I thought of it as a sort of research. Embedding myself with a kind of people I'd never lived around before, studying everything from the way they speak to the calluses on their hands which I was certain they all shared. Ryan accused me of romanticizing it. I told him that, with him, it's extremely hard not to.

As we drove down the path, surrounded by the high-reaching grass, I began to hear the wildlife channel-like noises of water and bugs, and a low, dull, mysterious and glottal hum.

"The fuck is that?" I asked, hating how panicked my voice sounded.

"Gators," Carlos and Ryan said, in perfect unison.

"I didn't know there was a swamp here…"

"It's South Carolina, bud. They're everywhere."

It seemed to me like a magical place. It had the capacity to be both dry and wet all at once, both comforting and frightening in equal measure. I wanted to reach across the seat and grab Ryan's hand, but I could still feel Carlos's eyes on me in the rearview, no doubt thinking of me as some naive New Yorker.

When the grass cleared, it gave way to a sprawling green yard, in the middle of which there was a massive house with the dreamlike wrap-around porch. I couldn't imagine what it must have been like, living here, coming home every day to something so huge and apparently splendorous. Beyond the clear green grass there were barns, sheds, fences. To the right of the property there were rows and rows of corn stalks. The whole place seemed alive with agriculture, and I tried not to look as awestruck as I felt.

The pathway finally turned to a well-packed gravel just outside the house, and Carlos parked the car in the hot sun. I guessed that, somehow, there were even more expensive cars in the garage. With a grunt of a goodbye, Carlos picked up all of our luggage and went inside. Ryan held me back by the arm.

One last kiss in our freedom. It felt, to me, like an apology. I, as ever, inferred from it what I wanted to. That he wished he could be honest with his father, that he wished, right now, that we could sneak away to some secret place where the grass was high and no one could hear us. But I choked up, and he pulled me toward the front steps instead.

Chapter Eight

In Wingdale, none of the floors are truly flat. Every building is old and poorly maintained, or at least, poorly maintained compared to the hardwood floors of the Meade farmhouse. Every plank shines, and none of the furniture rolls across the floor unprompted. Every surface is clean enough to eat off of, though no one would let you be that uncivilized. How funny, I thought, that they should be surrounded by animals but so opposed to acting like them.

The Meade family patriarch stood taller than me, and taller than his son. He shared Ryan's thick, sandy hair, but wore it parted down the center. He wore thin-rimmed glasses and a plaid shirt, tucked into his high-waisted, pleated khakis. At first glance he looked like a meek and mild man, but he betrayed my assumptions immediately, the moment he opened his mouth. He had the same commanding charisma as his son but lacked all his gentleness. He boomed like thunder from all the way across the house when he saw us enter through the front door. His footsteps seemed to shake the house. As well-kept as it was, it was still old and prone to being rickety.

"Son!" He spread his massive wingspan but didn't offer an embrace. I stood by, shrinking in on myself a little, collecting one of my elbows in my opposite hand, observing the strange father-son ritual I'd never gotten to experience. I hadn't been old enough. I was small enough that my father could still hug me without getting all weird about it. Not that he took advantage of the opportunity.

"Hey, Pop," Ryan said. His voice seemed to change to a deeper baritone in the presence of his father. I guessed, and maybe knew, that our voices are never the same in the presence of our parents.

"This is Lucas." He indicated me with another outstretched arm, and carefully placed a hand on my shoulder. Nothing like the heavy affection I'd grown used to.

Mr. Meade looked me up and down.

"We gotta get you out on the farm," he said. "Put some meat on them bones."

I laughed, if only because I guessed that was what he wanted. It seemed dangerous to do otherwise.

Mr. Meade retreated with no further questions, hobbling, yet somehow graceful, back into the mysterious labyrinth of the rest of the farmhouse. I turned to Ryan, waiting for him to say something almost apologetic. And I, full of sympathy, was ready to tell him he didn't have to.

He showed me where I would be staying. A room across the hall from his own, freshly painted in a sage green with country quilts on the bed. I sat on the mattress, noting its hardness, it's creaking. It seemed to cut through the newness of the place and remind me that this house was truly an old thing.

Ryan sat beside me, at a safe distance, as if his father had eyes in every room. His mother, I learned, was the ears of the operation.

"She can hear me *think* about masturbating," he said, though the serious look on his face betrayed any sense of joking. "And she'll just happen to need me to mow the lawn at that exact moment."

"Does she have a sixth sense about someone *else* wanting to touch your dick?" I asked, quiet as I could manage, raising my brow, trying to cling to our private routine. Again, he absolved me with his glorious laugh.

"Haven't tested it yet..."

As of right then, we were safe. He kissed me in a sad and nervous way, his lips rigid to remain quiet. In my insecurity, my instinct was to believe his frigidity was from a lack of love. But I thought of his father's eyes and his mother's ears and decided that he was simply afraid.

I soon found out that his father had not been kidding about getting me out on the farm. We were allowed a brief snack and a glass of sour lemonade before we were sent to the chicken coup, laden with scraps of food and gallons of water, as well as baskets for collecting eggs.

I was largely useless, trying my best to follow Ryan's graceful lead. But watching him proved too distracting, and I soon found hungry chickens pecking at my skinny ankles, begging me for food. But the way he held each egg, the way he turned it over in his long fingers, checking for crack and imperfections...I had rarely seen those hands care for anything but me, and to watch that gentleness from afar warmed me from my toes to my teeth. He tossed the scraps, then he poured the water.

He knelt down then, the chickens gathering around him like the Messiah, and he smiled at them with a new gentleness. I couldn't stop myself, then, from wondering if I could watch him adore animals for the remainder of my sorry life. If we could go on long walks, sharing the burden of an eager dog pulling relentlessly at its leash. I parted my lips as if to ask if he ever had the same thoughts, but then I heard his father calling from the wraparound porch. We both turned swiftly, a testament to his power.

"Quit dawdling," he boomed. Ryan nodded at me with the workmanship of a farmhand, then. He seemed transformed by this place. But, as everywhere else, he looked like he belonged. I finally understood the strength of his arms and the way sweat made him only more pristine.

We gathered up our baskets and buckets and began the journey back to the house, and I wondered what task Mr. Meade had in store for us next. Maybe, I figured, he was going easy on me, putting us on chicken duty. But in the distance, I saw the stables, the cow pen, and a shed that seemed to emanate the mournful sensation of death. Ryan's eyes flickered toward it, back and forth, his lips twisting into a foreboding frown.

"It's exactly what you think it is, bud," he told me quietly. I felt honored that he could read me so easily. "Slaughterin' shed."

I wondered if his kindness toward the chickens was little more than an apology. Preemptive, for when he had to cut off their delicate heads.

But our next task was not one so violent. We were sent out into the corn fields, and I made a joke about looking for crop circles, to which Mr. Meade reacted poorly, if what he did could be called a reaction at all. He simply looked at me with the notable absence of amusement. I gulped and stuffed my hands into the pockets of my cuffed denim shorts. I felt such a need to impress him like this was any old meeting-of-the-parents, like I was a boyfriend up against the life-altering challenge of a father. But as far as he knew, I was just some guy, and one on which the jury seemed to still be very much out.

I followed Ryan to the corn fields, marveling at how the stalks seemed to reach so high above our heads. Beneath the stalks and beneath his father, Ryan seemed to look small for the first time. I felt comforted by the fact that, even though the rose-colored glasses were surely gone from my face, I loved him even when he was subject to someone else's control.

Once out of view, he reached for my hand. Our arms swung between us, and we held onto one another as we traversed the uneven ground. It was drier there than in the driveway, but still there were pockets of water to avoid. Eventually, once our baskets were half-full of husk-covered corn, we came upon a clearing.

"Aliens?" I asked, still clinging to the hope that I had managed to be charming, at least to Ryan. And, easing my shoulders, he laughed.

"Sorry about pop," he said, placing his basket down on the ground. He released my hand and put his own on his hips, bending his back in a stretch toward the sun. "He ain't suspicious or anything." His accent was thicker, now that we were so far South. I found it adorable, but I didn't say anything. "Just got a thick shell."

"Then how'd you end up being so sweet?" I asked, following suit and putting down my own basket.

He stared out into the vista, and I wondered where their property ended. He sighed.

"Saw my mom bein' sad all the time. Figured that, if I were to be with someone, I'd want them to be happy."

"She's sad?" I thought of Angela, wondering at the myriad kinds of sadness that women seemed to feel.

"It's why she's so uptight, I think," he told me, still staring out at the horizon. Then he turned to me with a somber smile. "...are you happy, Lucas?"

He so rarely used my name anymore. It disarmed me.

We kissed in the blazing sunshine. I let my skin burn for the sake of showing him that yes, I was, overwhelmingly and unerringly, happy.

I met Ryan's mother late in the evening, when we were sitting in the living room, cutting the silence with a marathon of reruns. Ryan's legs were hanging over the armrest, his head just barely grazing my shoulder. We had, in the span of one day, developed a sort of system where we could maintain just enough intimacy to satisfy the aching in our throats. But not too much, so that we could get away with it, and appear as so many people love to assume two men: just exceptionally good friends. It was agonizing to try and dull the tenderness in my eyes. I only hoped that Mrs. Meade had no sixth sense for love.

She seemed reticent about all things, her eyes traveling just briefly to her husband before each time she spoke. Eventually, she warmed up enough, and felt safe to ask me questions, the same ones Ryan had asked me months ago. What's your major, where are you from... And like Ryan, I could tell she was listening. Her eyes glazed over some when I told her I was studying to be a journalist, like she was afraid in the back of my head I was planning some exposé on agricultural superpowers. But she was polite and held her teacup on her lap with the same sturdiness the entire family seemed to share.

We made it a few nights without breaking the rules. But one warm evening, when we were sure Mr. and Mrs. Meade were deep in a whiskey-induced sleep, Ryan tip-toed into the guest room, wearing his pajamas. I recognized the shirt as my own, and I could tell by his face that he felt a bit sheepish about wearing it. But I welcomed him into my arms, thrilled to tuck my nose into his shoulder and smell myself on his skin.

It was a slow sort of love, that night, to keep quiet. I sucked him off with care, and I relished in having no other choice but to taste every glorious inch of him so thoroughly. And his struggle to keep quiet made me ravenous. I wanted to beg him to fuck me. I'd had that inspiration so many times before but had always managed to silence myself in the best way I knew how. When I had him throat-deep, my lips sweetly surrounding him as he throbbed, I couldn't stop myself from reaching beneath the waistband of my sweat shorts and touching myself in the same careful manner. I looked up to see him grin. Together we melted, and when he came, the fullness of it brought me there as well.

I felt the badness of it, the secrecy and stupidity of dirtying one's clothes from even the simplest of acts. It made me grin, and as I slipped them off and tossed them into the corner I'd designated as the laundry bin, I felt his eyes on me, admiring me in the dark light of the guest room. The moon shone through the blinds in airy slats, and I turned to look at him, half-illuminated, naked and strong, his cock wilting as it lay spent against his leg.

We stayed that way for a moment, drinking one another in, smiling in the defeated sort of way one does when you realize that your heart is owned by someone else.

I fell asleep naked beneath the sheets, my head on his chest. When I awoke in the early morning to the sound of roosters, he was gone.

We ate our breakfast in giddy silence, reeling still from the previous night's mischief. He had turned me into a troublemaker. I was no longer afraid.

Once full of fresh eggs and black coffee, which Mr. Meade had insisted was the only way to drink it, we were sent back out to work. I'd become, over the past few days, not terrible at lifting dry, scratchy bales of hay and carrying them to another place. Despite all of Ryan's explanations, I struggled to understand the logistics of the farm, the 'why' and 'what' of it. But gradually, his father seemed to be less disappointed in me, the more my scrawny arms ached in the evening.

And we continued our nightly crimes, taking turns sneaking across the hallway to be with one another. Some nights, we just talked. But, so enamored, it felt just as naughty, even though to Ryan's parents it might appear entirely acceptable. Just two incredibly good friends. But if they could hear our whispers, they wouldn't think so.

"...do you think we should get a place next semester?" I asked one night, too exhausted to keep it in. "Like, together?"

Ryan tapped his fingers on his chest as he lay on his back.

"Maybe."

I didn't push the subject. Despite all our closeness, still I felt our relationship was too tenuous to reach the stage where we could discuss the future, and maybe even argue about it. This was the farthest I'd ever gotten with someone before it all went to shit, and I was clinging to the honeymoon phase, hoping it would never end.

It was almost July when I saw my first slaughter. I had feared that the animal might look at me, its head lying on the chopping block, with its eyes full of fear, begging me to help it. But when Mr. Meade laid the turkey down, and I saw the grotesque thinness of its neck, I felt nothing. Its eyes were beady and dark. We ate it that night for dinner.

Chapter Nine

It was a great surprise to me, the depths of hierarchy in the American south, when it came to the richest landowners in Charleston. Everywhere we went, Ryan and his parents were recognized, and unlike some more humble celebrities, they seemed delighted by the attention. Or at least, Mr. and Mrs. Meade did. Ryan stayed behind them, beside me, waving apathetically at those who greeted them, those who asked them polite questions while maintaining a wide grin. Ryan explained to me one day, as we sat licking ice cream cones on the hot boardwalk of Folly Beach, that this was prime season for trying to impress his parents.

"The Fourth of July party's comin' up," he said. "Everyone wants to get invited." He ran his tongue around the edge of the waffle cone. He liked his vanilla with rainbow sprinkles. I had a chocolate and vanilla twist.

"Why's it such a big deal?" I asked.

"Lotsa reasons. People want their kids to work on the farm. They want a discount on eggs. Stupid shit."

I laughed, knowing there was probably more to it than that. Maybe partying with the Meade family was a status symbol, like a fancy car or an inground pool.

"Do I have to suck up to your parents or am I already invited?" I joked.

"If you want." He took one definitive lick of his ice cream and then looked at me. "I was thinkin' we could bail on it. Spend some...time together." He looked away then, suddenly shy at his own suggestiveness

"You think anyone will notice?" I asked, leaning to the side, trying to follow his errant gaze, keep it for my own.

"Not if history's any indication," he said. "They start hittin' the punch pretty early."

"So, you always sneak away? Every year?" I asked, hating my tone. Ryan gave me a devilish half-smile and absolved me with a teasing glance.

"Yeah, but never *with* anyone," he told me.

We made our pact then, to celebrate the holiday alone, out of sight of the drunken party. And the conversation was imbued with the depth of the promise to finally, in the most teenage and silly of terms, go all the way.

The waves called. We finished our ice cream and, ignoring the old adage about waiting fifteen minutes, walked eagerly to the water. Walking across the hot sand, I kept wanting to reach for him, to lazily hook a finger through one of his own. But his parents were nearby, beneath a large umbrella, drinking beer from a cooler and reading whatever it is that rich homophobes read. I didn't want to hedge my bets that they were so engrossed as not to notice us, so I folded my arms across my nearly concave chest instead. Despite all the farm work, I still managed to look frail.

The water was cold, even beneath the hot Southern sun. But once we'd stood in the surf for a while, up to our ankles, we finally began our descent toward the crests of the modest waves. The water was different down there than it was on the beaches of New York and Jersey. Bluer and less frigid. Or maybe, when I watched Ryan jump in time with the curving waves, he just made it seem more magical.

We treaded water near one another when the waves were high and stood with our toes curling into the sand when they were low. Ryan squinted toward the shore, looking for his parents from whatever vantage point to which the ocean had carried us. They must have been asleep, because when the next wave came, he leapt in time with its cresting, arms spread, and fell into me with a playful embrace.

I used to be afraid of drowning. But beneath the water, our limbs entwined, I felt my lungs could withstand hours of stillness.

When we breached, we laughed. We stayed close, his arms over my shoulders, my hands on his hips, just above the waistband of his swim trunks. We glistened with salt water and the hot sun. Pressed to him, I felt myself pulsate with the threat of a poorly-timed erection. Ryan must have noticed, because he bit his lip, and then looked to the approaching wave. Once the water was high enough, he reached down to run his hand up and down my dick, growing harder, and I felt so sick with love and desire.

But the ocean seemed to calm, and there could be no more cover for us. Giving up on fooling around, we went back to our boyish playing. I felt so free, laughing loud, smacking my palms into the water to send a wall of splashing water his way. Just very good friends.

Maybe that was it. Maybe no one I'd dated had ever really been my friend before.

We stayed at Folly Beach until sunset. In the back of the car, we allowed our hands to drift across the leather seats, touching just at the fingertips. We had over a month left before the semester started, over a month left of spending all day missing one another even though we were so close, and I felt as though we would never reach the end. Those late-night visits were divine, but my every pore felt like screaming out, in broad daylight, the unbearable joy I felt to know that I could have him.

I found solace in the horses. They, like me, seemed to have a lot to say that they couldn't, or weren't allowed to. In their case, though, it had been God keeping them quiet, in whom I still didn't believe. But wherever creatures came from, there were some of them whose eyes were full of knowledge. The horses knew. They'd seen us in the stables, fooling around for the brief amount of time we could get away with. The horses didn't care. And if they could talk, I think they would have said so.

The holiday approached fast, and even a week before, Carlos was already busying himself with the preparations. I watched from the sidelines as he and Ryan set up the massive white tent and the collapsible tables, having been deemed too inexperienced to be anything but a hindrance. And just like the party itself, Ryan and I set about planning our escape. He knew the guest list, the schedule of activities, and approximately how many drinks his father would have had at certain times a day. We discussed it as we hung the flag bunting on the wraparound porch.

"Lawn games at around 4 in the afternoon," he said as he reached high above his head, tacking down the fabric. "That gives us about an hour, but then they usually serve dinner, and we'll be expected."

"Will they come looking for us if we aren't there?" I asked, starting to become stressed by this, feeling like it was on par with the anxiety of navigating an airport or finishing a final project all in one night.

"Yeah, so we should leave before the lawn games," he said with absolute certainty. He sighed as he climbed down from the ladder, and I was glad to have him back at eye-level. "After lunch, when they're less drunk because they're full of hot dogs, when they're ready to get another load on."

"You're wasted as a poet," I told him, and he snorted in laughter. "Too much of a tactical genius. Just like Angela. You should rob banks together."

"Oh yeah, but this'll be my biggest heist ever. With the best payout."

I grinned, and, knowing we were alone, I snaked my arms around his waist, staying vigilant at the open windows of the house.

I should have been faster. I should have spit it out, that I loved him. But I hesitated for just too long, and we heard the awful crunching of gravel beneath work boots and scrambled away from one another as fast as we could.

Carlos stood in the driveway, a nest of hanging fairy lights tossed over his shoulder and looked at us with a knowing silence. Ryan turned pale as me.

"'Los…" His voice was sad and pleading.

Carlos stared up at us, silent, his face grim and judging. And then, mercifully, he laughed.

"I didn't see a god damn thing," he said. "You know I don't give a fuck about any of that."

Ryan and I both exhaled, loud and relieved.

"Thanks, 'Los," Ryan said as Carlos climbed the stairs, carrying with him the lights to hang on the back porch and the white tent. He just shrugged, apparently apathetic.

All that fear for nothing. If only it was always that easy.

When my mom had caught me with a boy, back when I was just sixteen, it was the only time I actually missed her complete lack of caring about what I did. Usually, her ignoring me made me bitter, but as she screamed at me and scared Freddie Marshall so bad he climbed out my bedroom window, I wished she would just leave me alone like always. But suddenly, she had cared very much. Enough to be ashamed of me. She softened with time, moving comfortably back into her routine of ignorance, but my stepfather was steadfast in his disapproval.

Thus, when Carlos simply walked away without another word, waving a hand at us to go on doing whatever we wanted, I felt a years-old tension leave my shoulders.

Chapter Ten

The morning of the Fourth of July, Ryan looked out at the massive yard and its patriotic decor, and he thanked God out loud for the weather. It did seem like some sort of providence, that the summer should save its best day for the day of the Meade party. Maybe that was another thing being wealthy got you.

Our plan was to make ourselves invisible, to interact with the party in such a way that no one might miss our presence. Have a drink or two of light champagne, talk only to one another, and evaporate into the afternoon without anyone paying us any mind.

And our endgame kept me anxious. I patted myself on the back for my forethought, making sure that the lube in my backpack sat right on the top of everything else in the smallest zipper-pocket. And I knew, because he'd told me, that Ryan had never done it with a man before. He'd barely done it with a woman, either, as he had found it so compulsory, he gave up before the nagging feeling of guilt could overtake him. Guilt that he didn't want it, guilt that he should commit the very same act that created him. But he seemed to smile when we talked about this, instead. I whispered to him one night about how he could have me, and how it was okay to be nervous, and how I could hardly wait to feel him inside of me, where he belonged.

Our excitement brimmed that morning. But his parents were so distracted by making every little detail about their party perfect that they hardly spoke to us. Our job was done; the beer was on ice and the decorations were up. We were no longer necessary, and for that, we were grateful.

I sipped some champagne in the early afternoon in a futile attempt to calm my nerves, as I was soon back to my fidgeting anyway. Ryan, too, seemed restless, always avoiding his mother, who fluttered back and forth between the backyard and the house like a frantic moth searching for light. It felt, again, like something I was not supposed to see. Watching him be nervous, watching his bashful half-smile appear and disappear.

Once the crowd grew and the house and yard were awash in an ocean of indistinct chatter, we eased a little bit. Ryan greeted all the necessary people, introducing me as his friend, but always while softly pressing his palm to my back in a way familiar to me only from our secret nights together. The hardest part was escaping the pale-white girls in their pale-pastel dresses, all drawn to Ryan with so much giggling and eyelash-fluttering, you would think their parents were trying to arrange a marriage. They were, at first, relentless, but seemed turned off by my constant presence. Eventually they floated back to their mothers and fathers and the low-fat macaroni salad beneath the tent, and we were free.

The sun was high and the house was empty. The party outside was reaching a peak of drunkenness, judging by the cheering, shouting, and screaming. As we stopped outside of the guest room, he apologized to me.

"Cindy Gilligan has been after me since we were kids," he said. "I forgot she would be here."

"It's okay," I assured him, leaning lazily into the door as it opened, walking backwards to my pile of belongings. "I don't blame her."

He rolled his eyes at me and then, grinning nervously, and made his way across the hall to his bedroom. I quickly followed, lube in my pocket and a lump in my throat.

The sight I came upon was so endearing, that lump seemed to rise and threaten to make me cry. He'd made his bed, he'd set a record to play, and I remembered it as one we'd listened to one long evening that lasted into the early morning, awake in the dorm, entwined and talking.

I heard the lock on his door click shut, sealing the deal. I felt so much younger than I was. But at the same time, I felt that years had passed, that I was standing in a room with someone I'd already loved for years. Someone I'd known for a long, long time, but never stopped finding him intoxicating. In any house, in any room, wherever we ended up, I knew he could render me helpless until I died.

With a heavy exhale, apparently tired of being coy, he rushed to me, surrounding my face with his strong hands, and kissed me in a way he'd not done in months. It was unbridled and wet, so unlike the careful quiet we'd started to grow used to. I utterly wilted, clinging then to his shoulders as if, should I let go, I would sink through the floor and into a lonesome abyss. His fingers traveled into my messy hair, tugging at the indelible knots, filling me with the sense memory of every time he'd stroked my head, every time he'd gripped it while approaching the edge of orgasm. All of our intimacies seemed to collect in my stomach then. They had built up, each of them, to this. At the critical mass of love, we could resist no longer.

He made quick work of exerting his dominance, and I was happy to be at his whim. As he pulled at the hem of my shirt, urging it upwards, he walked me toward his bed, where I fell with a telltale creak of the mattress. And he winced, and I went wide-eyed, looking toward the door and waiting to get caught.

But nothing came, and we fell back into our giddy grinning as he climbed on top of me, burrowing his hips between my parted legs. I sighed to feel him pressed against me, and I wrapped my arms around his back, slipping my fingers and palms up beneath his shirt, feeling the twitching muscle, the smooth, tan skin. I delighted just in holding him, kissing him, for a while. There was no need to rush. That, and I knew he was nervous. As if I weren't also trembling with anticipation, filled with a thousand fears as to how wrong it could go, how disappointing it might be. But I was too elated at the same time, to hesitate in giving myself over completely. I welcomed him with my open jaw, and I felt his warm, wet tongue pushing toward my throat, and I groaned into it, my fingers curling into his back, my hips tilting up, showing him what he'd managed to do to me.

Without tearing my lips away, I reached down between us and fumbled with the button and zipper of his jeans, desperate and whining for the feeling of his warm skin, stretched tight with want. And when I felt it, I couldn't help the happy whimper that came from my throat. It was muffled by his mouth, and I could feel him smiling against my lips. Not a proud, boasting smile, that he could bring such a sound out of me. But something sweet and glad, something that made me feel loved.

I needed to be close to him. Closer, somehow, as if there wasn't enough of him for me to devour. I abandoned his cock for my own fly, undoing it with muscle memory, freeing myself then to rub against him. He breathed down my throat, shivering at the feeling, and then began to descend upon my neck with a flurry of hard kisses. The ones that leave little marks on your skin. I wrapped one hand around both of us, jerking us both off in tandem, in rhythm with the way he breathed and kissed. In the distance, I could hear the vague sounds of a party that had forgotten us entirely.

We were safe and free, and it just felt so damn good. I looked down at where our bodies met and felt dizzy from the sight of it. Our two swollen heads pressed together, weeping just a little as I held them, stroked them, got us ready. And then, he reached beneath my chin and tilted my gaze back up to meet his.

"Luc…" His voice was throaty and breathless. He ran a thumb along my bottom lip.

"It's okay," I assured him, reading the uncertainty in his glassy eyes. "It's okay…" More quietly, more nurturing. And then, I give away how desperate I was to feel him inside of me. "Take off your pants."

He releases the smallest, most awestruck laugh, and then retreated just enough to be on his knees, pulling down his jeans with haste. I licked my lips when I saw his perfect cock in full, achingly hard and standing erect on its own. I didn't have much time to admire it, though, as he soon began pulling at my pants as well. He dragged them down my legs in a manner most careful, cautious of my knobby knees as if suddenly I was so fragile. He felt the bump in one of the pockets, dug out the bottle of lube, and I saw his face grow all the more flushed as he looked at it. I chuckled, and he laid it down beside us on the bed.

And then I lay there, naked, for him, and he pulled off his own shirt and tossed it aside. Just like the first time, when all this began, he looked at me as no one had before. I had, in the past, felt grotesque in my nudity, with my knees bent and spread, revealing every intimate and fragile part of myself. I had wanted to cover my eyes, and the eyes of whomever hovered above me.

But I welcomed him to look, to feel. I didn't beg for him to turn me over and avoid looking at my face. Instead, I reached for the little bottle, and I reached for his hand. First, I brought his fingers to my lips, ghosting kisses along his fingertips, allowing them just-so inside my mouth. And then, giving him permission, I placed the bottle against his palm and curled his fingers around it. He nodded, understanding, and held the bottle to his chest.

For someone unfamiliar, he seemed so naturally deft at it all. He watched the liquid drip from the bottle, onto his fingers, and then turned his attention back to me. Before he even touched me, which I so badly needed him to, he came back down for a kiss. It was then that I felt it, the cool sensation of wet fingers pressing just-so against my hole. I curled my arms around his neck, urging him to keep going. As he kissed me, and I kissed him, he timidly pressed one nervous finger inside me, just a little.

"That's good..." I told him, feeling the need to guide him. He didn't protest.

"Another?" he asked me, muffled in the briefest break in our kissing. I nodded.

At two fingers, he grew a little more confident. Sliding them in and out, slow at first, learning just how pliable my body was willing to be. And I tried my best to relax every muscle, to ease myself into the pleasure of it. His hands had always been something that managed to make me sweat. His veins, his knuckles. And now, having them where I'd long daydreamed, I finally understood the full rapture of them. I wanted more. I bared down on his hand a little, pulling him toward me, bringing my knees to my chest, allowing him whatever of me he wanted.

At three fingers, I was beginning to squirm, and he was beginning to breathe so shallow, so short. If I'd allowed myself to, I could have gotten lost in just this. But I knew that something greater was waiting, throbbing, twitching to be inside of me.

I grabbed his wrist and pulled his fingers out of me. Again, I gave him a subtle, quiet nod.

I poured some lube into my palm then, and wrapped my hand around his cock, urging him toward me, holding the tip against me, just where it needed to go. And as he hesitated there, I pumped my hand up and down, tilting my hips, begging for him.

It hurt at the start, as it always does. The brief stinging before the joy takes over. I gasped and gripped onto his hips when first he entered me, holding him still, keeping him from going in another further just yet. But then, exhaling, I dug my fingers into his skin and invited him closer, slid my hands around to his rear and pulled him to me. The shudder I heard from him told me that he'd really had no idea what to expect, that there was nothing that could have prepared him for the hot, tight feeling of fucking another man. His eyes even looked a bit wide, in some measure of shock, and his brows knitted together in a display of helplessness.

He kissed me again, soft like the first time, as if to balance out the hardness, the depth. My elbows shook as he slowly pushed himself all the way, as far as my body could take. I wished that there had been more of me. I wished that I could take everything he had.

Once we reached that tipping point, he was no longer so slow and shy. He began to move, in, out, grunting so quietly each time. I wanted to squeal, delighted by the straining feeling, the repeated little joy of feeling him push inside me past the tip of his cock.

He buried his head in my neck, and I smiled up at the ceiling.

We ground into one another, allowing ourselves the luxury of moaning, gasping, grunting, whispering one another's names in a hungry whimper. He mumbled into my skin how good it was, how tight it was, how perfect. I was sweating beneath him, feeling the blossom of release starting to form in me, feeling his erection grow even stiffer as we both approached climax. Maybe it was quick, and maybe it didn't shatter the earth. But when he came, when I felt those few final thrusts, it felt as though my body simply evaporated into pleasure. His shouting was so rough, so unhinged, like he couldn't control the noises he made. I begged, *yes, yes, yes, all of it*, my whining voice sounding on the verge of sobs.

It was silent when he collapsed onto me, when I wrapped my arms around him and let my knees straighten. The record had reached the end, and we lay in the quiet, breathing. I strained my eyes to glance at the clock. Our plan had been flawless, and the party was falling quiet with people getting ready to eat. But I had no desire to return to the crowd. Not yet.

Ryan, silently, rolled off of me and to the edge of the bed, reaching for a stray towel. I half-expected him to toss it to me, ask me to clean myself up. But he kissed my forehead, and he did it for me. He then tugged at one of the sheets we'd rendered into disarray and pulled it up over our heads. In our hiding place, we nestled close.

"That was…" He couldn't finish his thought with anything but an exasperated breath.

"Yeah," I agreed.

We dozed and talked, made plans for further mischief. The party grew loud again, and we groaned as we emerged from our lovers' bower.

Once clean, dressed, and misted with some sort of body spray to hide the smell of sex, we lazily walked together through the house. We leaned against each other as if we were the only thing keeping each other upright. And at the threshold, just before the sliding door that led to the back porch, we shared one last kiss. He laughed then, our foreheads pressed together and a hand on my cheek.

"Happy Fourth of July, I guess," he said. I snorted and it dissolved into hiccupping laughter, and by the time we made it through the door, we were back to pretending.

We were hardly greeted, as everyone seemed too inebriated to notice anything but the fact that their cup was empty. And we, not above giving into the atmosphere, ladled ourselves each a generous helping of punch. We toasted quietly, only us knowing to what it was.

Only us, and maybe Carlos, who stood at the other end of the tent, smiling slyly, raising his own glass and looking pointedly at us. I guessed then that *someone* had noticed our absence, and had maybe even run interference for the duration, on our behalf. Ryan and I raised our plastic cups at him, as well, and the three of us took a victorious sip.

When tipsy, it was a little harder to stay away from one another. At the sun set, Ryan had taken to leaning on me, his elbow on my shoulder in a way that could be mistaken for fraternal. Or maybe, just like I often did, people were more likely to see what they wanted to see.

Like Cindy Gilligan, who hung on us like a lemming until her sloshing stomach beckoned her to find a private shrub in which to empty itself by way of her throat. Or Mr. and Mrs. Meade, who paid us no mind in favor of dancing in a way that told me they might have, years ago, been truly in love.

When the party died down, and everyone began to disperse, we were left alone on the back porch with the dregs of the punch bowl all to ourselves. We sat out there until the sky turned periwinkle, the sun threatening to rise, holding hands between two wooden deck chairs, basking in the afterglow, even hours after we'd left his bed.

Before the roosters could catch us awake, we headed back inside and retreated each to our own rooms, regretfully settling back into the charade.

Chapter Eleven

In the late morning, after not a lot of sleep, I was still aglow. My body still seemed to vibrate with joy so much that I couldn't even feel truly tired. I was wide awake and eager, and I got out of bed with shaky knees and a bright grin. It was another sunny day, as I felt all days would be, and had to be, because right then the world seemed too perfect to be anything else.

Outside of the guest room, it seemed quiet. Given the time of day, I figured everyone was out working, building up their ravenous appetites for lunch, powering through their hangovers like a bull through a red cape. I could see the backyard from my window, how the tent flapped in the breeze and the lawn was littered with plastic cups. I had a feeling that would be my responsibility, but I didn't even groan at the prospect. I was still too giddy, every moment from the day before playing on a loop in my head. I wondered if each time would be like that, if my life from then on could be the sweet repetition of visions of love. The rose-colored glasses came back on.

After I dressed, I headed toward the kitchen, padding quietly in my socks to try and avoid being immediately put to work. I thought, if I were stealthy, I could at least have a peaceful cup of coffee, and maybe I could even sneak in some forbidden milk.

But I got partway down the hall, and I saw the tall shadows of men standing in the light that burst through the glass windows and doors. I felt I could recognize them, so distinct were the Meade men. Or maybe it was just the shape of him, of Ryan, stretching out impossibly across the hardwood floor. I would know him even by shadow, and it warmed me. I retreated just a little, trying to keep my own shadow from joining the scene. Mr. Meade's booming voice then filled the room.

"I just feel so embarrassed by this," he said, though he sounded more angry than ashamed.

"You?" I heard Ryan parry. "*You're* embarrassed?" He scoffed. My chest began to fill with worry and the sense of doom I had managed to shake off after all this time. "How the fuck do you think I feel?"

"You watch your tongue with me."

There was some heavy sighing, the sound of pacing back and forth as I watched the shadows glide across the floor.

"Knew I shouldn't have sent you to that damn New York school," Mr. Meade said. "Buncha damn libs gettin' my only son to experiment. What else goes on up there, son?"

"It's college, dad. I learn shit."

"Learn how to be a god damn homo, is what you learn."

"Dad--"

"I want that boy out of my house. I want you to cut that shit out. Embarrassing..." More silence. My heart ached, and I found myself pressing a hand into my bony chest as if that could stop the hurt. "I'll not have a god damn fa--"

"Dad." I had never heard Ryan's voice so deep, so hurt, so furious. I felt some measure of pride, hearing him that way. "I'm not a...one of those."

"...what do you mean you're not? One of our guests saw you fucking that boy, butt-ass naked, in front of God--"

"Well tell your friends to quit snooping," Ryan spat. "And I mean I just...it wasn't..."

"Wasn't what, boy?"

"I was just foolin' around, okay? He was game, so I did it, n' it ain't gonna happen again, alright?"

It was largely silent from the sunny kitchen, but in my head, it felt so loud. All the blood leaving me, sending me into a ghostly pallor. I leaned against the wall, wincing at how it creaked, remembering how very old this place was. Old and backwards. Everything seemed to invert and make me dizzy.

"You mean that?" Mr. Meade asked.

"Yeah, it's nothing. Just...a mistake, okay?"

I never knew Ryan to be a liar. I had never, to my knowledge, heard him say one untrue thing. And, the ground pulled out from underneath me, I knew then that he had to be telling the truth. I knew then that lying to Mr. Meade was a sin punishable by extreme means. My lungs felt empty.

Their conversation continued, too quiet for me to hear over the pounding of my own heart, my own panic. I stumbled back to the guest room in a haze, a fugue. I watched my skinny arms collect my belongings, watching my veiny hands stuff them, haphazard as ever, back into my bags. I did my best to abate the nausea.

I seemed to be carried by puppet strings. Just like I'd been drawn to Ryan. Just like I'd been drawn to that basement, to the South, into the ocean. Nothing, I realized, had ever been in my control. That's always the case when you're a god damn idiot.

I made my sloppy, daring escape through the window. As much as I wanted to fight, to yell, to beg him to tell me the truth, the puppet strings pulled me outdoors. They told me that every warm and tender feeling I'd gotten from him was there out of panic, obligation, and mere curiosity. I was an experiment, and a failed one.

And either way, Mr. Meade was going to kick me out. My dirty body and my dirty mind.

I landed in the grass and it stung from my ankles to my neck.

I rounded the house in a hurry, my eyes heavy with tears, threatening to burst forth in loud sobs, to give myself away, reveal me as the pathetic person I felt I was. Wouldn't that just make Mr. Meade so happy; to know for sure I was the stereotype he wanted me to be? Sensitive and feminine, in love with a straight man, beguiling him into bed like a predator? I felt sick inside.

I ran across the field, back toward the entrance to the swamp, where I could finally disappear. I wanted to be entirely invisible. If I no longer had a body, there would be nowhere for the shame to stay.

The walk back through the swamp seemed infinite. Like love or a dark, moldy hallway. The ground was permanently saturated, made of mud, staining the bottoms of my shoes in a black-brown. I kept turning my head, squinting toward the narrowing vista of the Meade family farm. As if I might see him, or Carlos's Cadillac, rumbling along the uneven ground to retrieve me.

But the sun kept getting lower in the sky, and no one came. I gave him countless excuses. His father, his mother. Maybe, finally, he had decided that ghosts do exist, and they were rumored to haunt the swamp. Anything but what I felt, in my heart, was true. That what he'd said had been real, that he cared more for his father's opinion than for me.

And yet I kept looking back. What was that Bible story? Ryan would know it. His father would know it better.

No shouting, no Cadillac. Just the frogs and the alligators, animals somehow more grotesque than how I managed to feel.

My shoulders ached with the weight of my overstuffed backpack. I felt weaker than ever, my stomach growling for the great and heartiness I'd grown used to over the past month. I realized then how many things I would have to say goodbye to. Not just Ryan, but so many of the places and things next to which he looked so perfect. But even if he were to follow me, I knew, he would continue to awe me.

It would be easier to hate him for not rushing down the muddy pathway to my side. At least in theory.

The animals just couldn't be loud enough. I wanted them to scream above the echo of the conversation I overheard, repeating in my head.

When I finally reached the main road, the sun was down. I looked left and right, searching for anything familiar. It occurred to me then, even when we had left the farm and gone out, I'd made no effort to orient myself. I'd simply allowed myself to ease into the thick Southern air, allowed myself to become disoriented in love and heat. Maybe Ryan had made me stupid, more than he had made me strong. I wasn't brave anymore. I wanted to smoke, and to cower in the grassy edges of the road to hide from anyone who might drive by and see me. Neither direction looked like it might lead to a bus station, and I had no money either way.

I felt like I was always out of my own control. I watched myself lift one skinny arm and hand, leaving one foolish thumb erect toward the road.

A stranger might either help me or kill me, and at that moment I couldn't decide which one I would prefer.

***

My skin began to burn in the hot sun, my begging thumb aching from remaining upright. Countless cars passed me. None of them had the shine and opulence of Carlos's Cadillac, the mysterious wealth of one of the ones in the Meade garage. The sun seemed to dry my tears before I could even cry them. I was glad of my stoniness, as it kept me looking somewhat sane, as if that might help, might make someone stop and help me.

By the time the sun started to skim the horizon, a station wagon ground to a halt along the gravel shoulder of the endless road. I gulped, resigning myself to whatever awaited me. I looked for the shine of a knife or a gun through the window, the grim eyes of someone on the hunt for an easy kill. And wouldn't it be? I'd not eaten since the party; I was swaying where I stood. As if, even at my best, I would have stood a chance.

The window rolled down with a struggle. I saw the man in the driver's seat, bobbing, turning the crank on the ancient door. He was young, maybe thirty or so, and a woman sat beside him in the passenger's seat.

"Everything okay, bud?"

It was then that I cried. Unable to speak, I covered my face with my hands, beginning to blubber like a child, no doubt bewildering these two strangers. I figured they would drive away.

But all I heard was a car door open and shut. I looked through a small crack between my skinny fingers, and I saw the woman rounding the car. She looked tired but glowing, tan from the sun, her hair tied up in a ponytail behind the halo of flyaways that surrounded her head.

She had the strong arms of someone who'd been through worse than me. When she wrapped them around me, I shuddered out a desperate breath. It was how one ought to be held when they were a child, in a way I'd forgotten, if it ever happened in the first place. And, too weak to resist, I allowed myself to regress.

"It's alright, kid," she told me. Maybe in some other circumstance, were the world not ending, her calm voice might have bid me to believe her. "We'll get you where you need to go."

Chapter Twelve

By the time we made it up North, my spine had changed shape in order to comfortably rest on the leather backseat of a station wagon. My drifter friends had been kind, and had listened to my sob story, and then told me their own. They were like a copper-stealing Bonnie and Clyde, on the run with a wad of cash hidden beneath the carpet floor of the wagon.

There was a constant worry in my heart, that things would turn sour. That I'd find out they dealt drugs or planned to kill me, or that we'd get involved in some sort of gang violence that I most certainly was not cut out for.

But everything was calm. It was just long drives, hot days, cheap beer in cans, cracked open as we all sat in the back-hatch. We got to know one another, and I felt like so much less of a coward, being in the presence of criminals. They never made me feel like I was anything less than brave, like them. Walking alone up a road, ready to face the cruel and unfamiliar world because my heart had been broken. Bonnie said I should write a book about it, or something. I told her I didn't have the determination to do anything like that. She told me I was full of shit.

I remembered some of the sights on the drive up, having seen them on the way down, early in the summer, traveling to my doom with Ryan at my side. The memories stung deep. I couldn't look at anything without being reminded of him in one way or another. The world was too full of him, and no matter where I went, I feared, I would never get away.

The sights became even more familiar once we made it across the border into New York. They marveled at seeing the big city from the freeway, tracing the high-reaching skyline with their eyes as I drove. It was my turn, and they were a little bit afraid of the traffic. I followed my muscle memory of the state, turns and off-ramps taking me home as I stayed below the speed limit, putting it off for as long as I possibly could.

We pulled up in front of my mother's house, still half-painted from a project started years ago.

"You sure this is where you wanna be?" Bonnie asked me.

I thought about my other options. I thought about Angela, about her family, and about how nowhere I could sleep would ever feel like a home, but this was the closest thing. I thought about how much it might hurt to go inside that house and felt like I deserved whatever awaited me.

"Yeah," I said.

Our goodbye was long. Clyde wept. I thanked them for not being serial killers and gave them one last chance to change their minds on that.

And like always, no one laughed.

I knocked on the door, knowing for certain that the doorbell would still be defunct, left unfixed like the paint and the wiring and every other little thing my stepdad never got around to. The constant running of the downstairs toilet, the agonizing slow drip of the kitchen sink. My mother, still sad, even though she claimed he made her happy.

She answered the door in a terry cloth robe and slippers. And, to my shock, she seemed overcome with some maternal instinct, that thing she'd been fighting off since I was born, and she took me into her arms like I was a child who had scraped his knee. It felt nothing like how Bonnie had held me. Every back ache I had put off while sleeping in the backseat seemed to come rushing in all at once, tightening their grip of my spine.

I had cried so much the past few days it felt like I had nothing left. I had been wrung out entirely. I heard the drip of the sink, and I felt so thirsty for something other than beer.

"What's going on, honey?" she asked. She retreated from our embrace, holding my arms in her hands, looking up at me, waiting to hear the worst.

I heard the heavy footsteps that had always made me shiver. My stepdad, somehow taller than me, and his slow ambling through the house.

"Who's at the door?" he yelled, sounding angry already, as though any visitor would be a great inconvenience to him. He saw me, and his thick eyebrows shot toward the sky. "Oh, well if it isn't the journalist."

He pronounced it *join-a-list*.

He clapped me on the back like always, his best attempt at affection, and then took in a deep breath and retreated to the basement. He could only tolerate so much of me.

I was allowed to nap in what had once been my room, my mother taking my clothes to put them in the wash, to cleanse the sweat and the South out of them. Showered and clean for the first time in days, I collapsed onto the stiff bed, and groaned in an almost happy little way, that it wasn't made of sticky leather, and that the room was free from the admittedly charming banter of two uneducated drifters in the front seat. I plugged in my long-dead phone and found no attempts at contact.

My head hit the pillow. I fell asleep immediately. I was afraid to let it happen. I was afraid to dream. In my dreams, it hadn't happened. In my dreams Ryan was beside me, and I'd not cried at all, and I wasn't in this cold and sterile bed in a house I hated, full of bad memories.

But my body was too tired to last. I had a long, sweet dream where Ryan loved me. The summer lasted forever, and every night was a well-lit party from which we were permitted to escape. But then I woke up, and the summer heat was soaking through my clothes, and I was alone. I understood, then, why some people want to sleep forever.

Even at my lowest, I'd wanted to live. And I knew, even though I was a hypocrite, that living for the love of a man was stupid. But before him, none of my dreams had been so sweet. I had no incentive to keep on sleeping until then.

In my dream I was still in a bed. A bed I'd never seen nor slept in before. In my dream bed, Ryan's body was curled around my own, the sun rising in the clear pane of a wide window. He was talking, but I couldn't make out what he was saying. I couldn't hear him, and I couldn't hang onto the dream no matter how hard I tried. I still woke up, and I still had to deal with reality.

I was forced to explain myself in the living room, my mother listening with pursed lips, my stepdad zoning in and out depending on how disappointing I was coming off. He would tune back in whenever the story hinged on my own mistakes.

"Well, I guess it was bound to happen," my mother said. "Things just aren't meant to be."

"I don't believe in that sort of thinking." Nothing, in my mind, was meant to be anything. Everything just *was*. And everything was shitty.

"No, I mean, between two boys," she clarified. "It always ends between you."

I stared blankly, my mouth hanging open. I could have spat some venom, told her that being straight didn't mean anything, given her track record of divorce and poor choices in men. I could have told her that maybe if she slept with another woman, she might not be so god damn uptight. I could have stormed out, back into uncertainty, belonging nowhere still.

But I didn't. I just cried. For weeks on end, becoming insufferable. I stalked the house like a gaunt specter, wailing in the night. My mother and stepfather insisted I would get over it, just like I did every prior breakup, every prior devastation that had proven to be something easy to forget. But I couldn't explain how this was different, how Ryan had made me sleepless into the early morning like no one ever had before, how he looked at me that day, when I felt beautiful for the first time. I assumed that she wouldn't understand. And not just because it was Ryan. I was certain no love had ever been like ours or had ever felt real like ours. I had nothing to compare it to that even came close. No prior relationship, no perspective of my mother's marriages that could make me look at what Ryan and I shared without a sense of wonder, and a certainty that nothing and no one would ever make me feel that way again.

Eventually I stopped checking my phone. Eventually I stopped crying and started writing. There was so much inside of me. So much I'd seen that I had tried to ignore for the sake of not being reminded of him.

I felt like some sort of eccentric recluse, locking myself in the guest room, its depressive energy seeming to radiate through the house, gathering empty water bottles and used napkins and unwashed plates. I settled back into the old shameful routine, avoiding my mother and stepfather, skirting around them as if, should I shrink myself enough, they might not see me. And shrink I did. Impossibly thin, but in flux from nights spent up late devouring pizza bagels like a child. And when I should catch my mother's attention, it was only for her to scold me like always.

But I no longer had earlier youth to cling to. I had no more excuse to be irresponsible and sloppy, other than heartbreak that neither she nor my stepfather understood. Therefore, in their eyes, I had even less of a reason to be such a piece of shit. Not that it stopped me. Not even the perfect summer weather and the many invitations from my old friends to go back to the basements in which we used to party. None of it enticed me out of the pit I'd dug for myself.

I had hoped that, being indoors and far away from Ryan, nothing could remind me of him anymore. But he followed me even into places he had never been. The color of something, so like his eyes. The sound of a man's voice on the television, saying something even remotely similar to something he'd said to me, once. A song I'd heard, a shirt I wore that I remembered him peeling off of me some perfect evening.

And despite my sinking depression, back with a vengeance, every time there came a knock at the door, I would sit up straight and find myself filled with a foolish hope that Ryan might be on the other side. It was as if I yearned to be disappointed, as much as I yearned for sleep when I could have those perfect dreams of him, his touch, his voice.

Eventually, once my apathy had overtaken my sense of hope, my stepdad fixed the doorbell. Its sound was somehow more jarring than the rough rapping on the old wooden door. Alone in the house, I jumped at the ringing that managed to permeate every wall. I groaned, splaying myself out on my bed in a refusal to participate. But the ringing kept on coming, in an enraging litany, and I threw a pillow at my window to get them to stop.

"Shut up..." I mumbled, my voice hoarse from how little I'd spoken of late. The ringing stopped for a moment, and I closed my eyes, satisfied that I'd driven them off, but then the barrage started anew. "Come *on!*"

I took my time getting to the door, walking and pouting my way down the stairs. I prepared myself for the worst, for having to fight off religious fanatics that would only remind me that not everyone could be a person of faith with the grace and understanding that Ryan did. Not everyone, and in fact maybe no one, could look at the world the same way he did.

I opened the door slowly, allowing it to make the awful creak that my mother continued to pester my stepfather about, wanting to make this place feel as dry and cracking as my own skin.

Instead of getting a pamphlet or a bible shoved in my face, I was met with something far more threatening.

Chapter Thirteen

"You, asshole," Angela said.

She stood on the stoop with her arms folded across her chest, familiar fire in her eyes and her foot tapping on the concrete. I was sure she was correct in her insult, but there were so many things I'd done wrong, I couldn't decide which one she'd come here to berate me for.

"You gonna let me in?" she asked with a raise of her eyebrows. Usually, in the summertime, Angela seemed aglow with relaxation and ease. But now, standing beneath the tiny awning, she seemed just as stressed as she'd been during every finals week we've ever shared.

"Are you gonna kill me?" I parried, though I did stand aside to let her walk past me.

"Dunno yet," she admitted. I closed the door as she slipped out of her shoes, ever-polite, even though my mother wasn't home. "Depends on what you have to say for yourself, Luc."

"What are you talking about?" I asked, climbing the stairs with that same slump in my shoulders, beckoning her, should she want to follow, into the living room. It too had suffered some of my sloth, and Angela instinctually put one of the empty cups on top of a coaster, leaving behind an unseemly ring, at which she frowned.

"Don't be a dumbass," she scolded me. "It's about Ryan."

To hear the name out loud, for the first time in what felt like ages, made my chest ache. I groaned and laid down on one of the couches with a flop.

"I'm sorry I didn't call you or anything, it hurt too much to talk about--"

"That's another grievance for another time." I could tell by the venom in her voice that yes, she was angry with me for seemingly dropping off the face of the planet, but that wasn't why she was here. She would deal with her own hurt, her own ramifications of me being a shitty friend, later. It was almost selfless of her. "What I wanna know is why you left that boy all by himself down in the Deep South without saying goodbye. He emailed me, hysterical."

I raised my hands into the air, exasperated.

"So, he contacted *you*."

"Would you stop that?" she asked me, batting my skinny leg with the back of her hand. "Bein' all bitter when you got no right. Why'd you just leave like that?"

I sighed and stared at the ceiling.

"He didn't tell you what he said? To his dad?"

"He sure as hell did," she told me, defiant. "He told me that he tried lying to him, saying it didn't mean nothing--"

"Huh?"

"--and then soon after he broke down, came out to his parents, n' then got booted from the house."

"He did...?"

"They snapped his phone in half, made him pack his bags, kicked him out. He emailed me from a library."

"...Oh."

"'*Oh,*'" she mocked, shaking her head. "He went to go find you, and take you with him, but you'd already left. Like an asshole. He's been staying with me, having a fuckin' crisis." She looked around the room, apparently aware that I was in a crisis of my own. I searched her eyes for sympathy.

I felt ten kinds of conflicted. Angry with Ryan's parents, angry with Ryan for not reaching out to me, angry with Angela, angry with myself. Touched that I was apparently worth getting kicked out of the house for, ashamed at the pride I felt for that. Apparently, I was quiet for too long because Angela nudged me again.

"Why did he go to you?" I asked meekly. "Instead of me?"

"Because," she began, as if the answer should have been obvious. "You never gave him your damn address."

Every battling emotion seemed to then convene on guilt. I could feel no joy at the possibility that he missed me. At least, I thought, I wasn't *that* much of an asshole. I sat up, rested my elbows on my knees and my head in my hands. Angela seemed to soften then, and moved over to set beside me, a hand on my hunched back.

"He doesn't know I came here," she admitted. "I just had to see for myself what kind of shit you've been up to."

I motioned to the empty house.

"Mhm," she said, rubbing my back. "You need to get off your ass, Luc. Semester starts in two weeks, have you even registered for classes?"

I shook my head. The prospect of learning anything had seemed too much for my already busy, seemingly deteriorating mind.

"Come on," she said, hooking one arm through mine, pulling me up from the couch. "Let's get your shit together." I was subject to her whim, too weak to fight. Too aware of how right she was to bother protesting. All her old gentleness, that power she spared only for those she deemed had earned it, came back, and her eyes softened on me. Even if it were pity, even if it weren't sympathy, I had to take what I could get. I had to grab onto anything that might save me.

As we walked to my bedroom, we leaned our heads toward one another. A peace treaty of sorts, to show that even though I was an asshole and she was cruel, we would still forgive one another no matter what. I wondered if Ryan was the sort to forgive, and what it might cost me, if I ever saw him again. Shouldn't his God make him want to forgive and forget? Does that concept still apply if it hurts too bad?

I picked up the dirty plates from around my room as she registered me for classes for my penultimate semester. She recycled all the empty water bottles as I shaved the patchy stubble from my face. I began to feel and look a little more like a person.

I knew that it wouldn't fix me and knew that I had a long road of healing ahead of me. I knew that my mood and my lack of motivation wouldn't magically turn around once I felt clean and brave enough to contact Ryan. But it was a start. I don't think I could have even *started* if it weren't for that possibility.

We came to the reluctant agreement that it was a little too late for me to find other housing, either on campus or off. My mother, after some conniving yet gentle convincing on the part of Angela, agreed to let me stay rent-free as long as my room stayed clean and I didn't drop out. There was another, perhaps unspoken agreement, that I'd not be bringing any boys back to her home. But based on my behavior over the summer and my almost emaciated appearance, she didn't really seem to think it would be an issue.

Together, secretly, even once she returned to her house, Angela and I hatched a plan. There could be no plan flawless enough, and no action worthy of fixing what had gone wrong. There was nothing I could do to go back in time, wait just a little longer in that hallway that fateful morning, take Ryan with me up the coast after telling his dad to go fuck himself, so on and so forth. Nothing could return us to the perfect little joy we had.

But I needed something close to it. I needed to start again, and start with honesty, and return the favor of him sweeping me off my feet. I only hoped that I was capable.

Chapter Fourteen

The night before move-in day, the campus quiet and still as if it had just been condemned and abandoned all those years ago, I stood once again outside of the old science building, fidgeting with my shirt. Tucked in, untucked, tucked in. Nothing felt right. It wouldn't feel right until he was there.

Even after we'd swept the hallway, trapped and exiled the rats, scrubbed the floors until they shined like new in the weeks preceding the start of the semester, the long hallway seemed empty without him. It was as if the only way to walk down these halls was with him.

Since the electricity was long defunct in that building, we resorted to little lanterns, spread at equal distances down the length of the hall, to an old boom box with a tape deck to fill the hallway with music.

I was dressed no better than usual, though I'd managed to put on a little bit of weight so as not to appear as a ghost when he first saw me. I didn't need to frighten him any more than I already had. And I wanted to appear as much like myself as I could, as much as the way he'd last seen me. I didn't want to lie and act as though I was some different, better, more stable man. I wanted to be loved as I was. I wanted to love him as he was.

Angela lured him there under the guise of another evening that promised to be filled with fright, as she had promised that there were more classrooms to explore, more horrors to discover. And in his ever-adventurous spirit, he'd accepted.

"He didn't want to, at first. Just in case it made him think of you," she told me. "But I told him to get over himself."

He was not the one who needed that sort of harsh advice, and we both knew it.

But still, we did our best to make it look like a place where two people might be in love. We burned sage and vanilla candles from the dollar store, made an old-fashioned mixtape as if we were kids in the 1980s, breaking into this place to look for ghosts and prove our mettle to our peers. And eventually, after so much stealth and effort, it had become almost beautiful.

I stayed inside, in the middle of the hallway next to one of the lanterns, growing nervous. I decided, then, to blame it on a newfound fear of ghosts, and not on the actual terror I felt: the anxiety of seeing him again. Once I heard the heavy metal door begin to creak open, I knelt down and pressed *play* on the tape deck. It was that same old song, the one from the year before, when first I laid eyes upon him, stunned and already feeling guilt like a premonition of what was to come.

It was surprisingly full and loud, the sound from the tape deck. I took a steadying breath and watched as his divine shadow began to stretch out across the tile floor. The last time I'd seen it, I had felt my chest cave in one itself. And now, I felt it bursting with love.

He even seemed to flinch a little when the door closed behind him, its sound echoing even over the music. Gulping, willing my feet to leave the floor, arms stiff at my sides, I began my approach, coming further into the light, showing him that I wasn't an illusion.

His hair had grown a little longer. His skin had gone a little pale from being sequestered in Angela's house. He had become a little soft on her mother's cooking. But still, even though he was changing shape and looked somewhat gaunt and sad, I overflowed with an immediate desire. His shoulders sank, and so did mine. I felt deathly afraid, trying to read him, trying to discern if the shivering look on his face was full of disdain, or fury, or the love that would finally absolve me.

Once we were close, I wanted to reach for him. But I stayed still, terrified of being turned away.

"What is this?" he asked, and his voice made my toes curl in my shoes.

"An apology," I told him. "For...all the shit."

He snorted. Again, I could not read him, if he felt humored, or in disbelief that I actually thought I could even begin to mend things between us.

"Woulda been better if you'd just...not left me," he said, frank but coy. "Then you wouldn't have had to kill a bunch a' rats or whatever..."

"...I would kill so many rats, Ryan," I found myself saying, as if it could measure up to the sort of promises I wanted to make to him. "I would--" It was too late, and I was running with it. "--I would literally become a fucking exterminator, Ryan, I feel so fucking..." My voice shook, that ever-present lump in my throat rising. I saw him smile, as if unwilling, trying not to laugh even though he still looked so despairing. Bravely, I reached for his hands. When He did not pull them away, I brought them to my chest, and tried with all my might to look into his eyes in the dark. Before I could speak, he cut me off.

"Why's it so hard for you to be loved, bud?" he asked. My lips hung open and quivered. I felt more tears welling up behind my eyes, and I curled my fingers more firmly around his warm, warm hands.

"I--" I didn't know. I thought that, since I wanted it so desperately, it ought to be easy for me. I ought to have just been glad, and accepted it, and believed it and asked for it without shame. But I didn't. I ran away and searched desperately for any reason to tell myself he didn't love me. If I had just stayed, if I had just listened... "I don't know."

Ryan took a deep breath. I waited for him to tear his hands away, to leave. But he stayed. He did what I couldn't do.

"...I'm still angry with you," he admitted. "And we have a lot to talk about, but I..." He sniffed, apparently holding in just as much as I was managing to. "Goddammit, Luc..."

He kissed me then, always timed so perfectly, as the music reached its crescendo. I had expected, if I was so lucky as for this to happen, to burst into tears at all the weeks of lost time. Thinking of the long summer and how I could have been with him, could have been happy and not wasting away in something that used to be my home.

But all I could feel was joy. The regret could come later, I decided. After we made love, after we talked, after we were forced to deal with all the hurt we'd shared, all the hurt we'd caused. We could stay in this happy limbo for just a little while longer.

That night we made love in the old abandoned building, my back pushed against the wall. No matter how much we had cleaned it, still it seemed to retain its film of dust. In our movement, in our rutting, it filled the air in a fine mist, reflecting the glow of the lanterns.

It was a rushed sort of thing. It felt as though we were running out of time, somehow. That we absolutely had to be one with one another, in that instant, lest we get pulled away indefinitely in opposite directions. I clung to his back all the while, even as he pushed his shaking fingers into me. He held me in his still-strong arms, against the wall, and I did not worry that I would come falling to the ground.

He made quick work of lubing me up, sloppily, wet and dripping to the tile floor beneath us, as if there was no concept of wastefulness in that moment. We even laughed in that old gentle way, comfortable in the inherent silliness of sex. How, even though it was beautiful and romantic, there was no escaping the well-bred shame of the human body. He looked into my glassy eyes as he pressed his cock against my hole, the teasing feeling of it making me melt. As soon as he entered me, I fell apart. I whined like some sort of wounded animal, pawing at him to come closer, to go harder, to never relent and to split me apart with his love. I mumbled so many quiet apologies into his ear, burning red-hot against my lips.

When we came, it echoed down the hall. I felt that we had cured this place of its wretchedness. Ryan, with his faith and his love, blessing away all of the cruelty that once took place. In our panting and smiling and groaning we made the sun come up. We made the rays shine off of the tile floors.

I drove back to my mother's house in the morning. I came inside, and she was awake, having been prepared to glower at me no doubt since sunrise.

"Where have you been?" she asked.

I stared at her from the bottom of the stairs, weighing my options.

"With my boyfriend, mom," I told her. There was poison in my voice I'd been nursing for years. "See? Sometimes it does work out."

I laid in bed but I didn't sleep. All I could do was grin beneath the covers, my phone constantly alight with sweet, sleepless messages sent from just a few miles away.

Our trio returned to its previous routine. Scraping by with our grades, eating poorly and drinking cheaply, sitting in a neat little row on Ryan's dormitory bed each night. Angela, eventually and always, grew somber and excused herself as a third wheel. And then it would just be us, in so teenage a position, our knees bent and our backs against the painted cement wall.

After a few fun nights of ignoring the problem, I was finally the one to take the dive.

"I'm really sorry," I told him, my head on his shoulder, trying to keep my voice from sounding too tearful, lest I garner any pity that I didn't deserve. The honesty was sobering, and I felt his body tense beside me.

"I know, bud," he said. I smiled. I knew that typically it was easier, when apologized to, to reply that it was okay, not to worry about it, there was no harm done. But that would not have absolved me the way Ryan always could. He could never absolve me by lying. It wasn't okay and it would hurt for a while, but he knew I was sorry, and I knew he was sorry.

"Do you miss your family?" I asked, having been avoiding that, as well. He shrugged, pursing his lips to the side, and crossed his legs at the ankles, wrapping his knees up in his arms.

"I think I miss what I wanted 'em to be," he told me. "I guess part of me thought, n' it's stupid, I know, that I could come out and because it was me comin' out, he would suddenly get it."

"It's not stupid."

"It's alright, it is. You met him," he says, and manages to laugh.

"He's missing out on someone wonderful."

I saw Ryan grin, and even in the dim light from his desk lamp I saw his cheeks and ears turn a little pink. I had never been able to make someone so giddy before.

"Sweet talker," he accused me, though his tone was so gentle.

"Look…" I began, not entirely sure of what pep talk I was prepared to give, if any. I took one of his hands in mine and laced our fingers together. "Maybe he'll come around. It's not your job to convince him to, though."

"I know," he said with a heavy sigh. He inhaled, short and sharp, and then exhaled with no other sound. He did it again, and then he raised his head to look at me. "I love you."

"I love you too," I said, and it flowed from me so naturally you'd think we'd been saying it for years and years. It didn't frighten me, and it didn't make me feel the least bit uncertain. It just fell into place, like our bodies, like our voices.

We made so many plans and promises, that night and every night after. How we'd get a place of our own, how we'd move to the city, how we'd get a kitchen table with barstool chairs, and one day we would have the money and a yard for a dog. We collected an unwritten, lengthy list of things we wanted to do, together, to fill the years.

It ought to have been scary, to make those promises just on the edge of our real adulthood. But I knew that I meant it. I knew that I could never be dishonest or a coward ever again.

Epilogue

It is the end of another long, slow summer. The kind that has managed to go on uninterrupted, unfettered. A summer three years after the worst of our lives, miles away from the epicenter. A summer on some other eleventh floor, in some nicer building, in some city we've both been dreaming of forever. Even high up, in New York, you can never feel as though you're in the sky. The world below is far too busy and loud. No amount of fog or orange-tinted sunset could make you believe you were anywhere else. And we don't want to be.

It has been an unseasonably cool August, and we are so keen on remaining happy, we have ignored the reasons why and simply chosen to keep our windows open and let the breezes wake us. There are only two weeks left before it is back to our slightly less idyllic reality. But even when we're not permitted to laze around and do as we please, our life together fits into the plans and promises we made years ago, back before we had the means to make them happen.

After graduation, I had finally managed to sit down and edit that piece I'd written in the squalor of my mom's guest room. From all that rot there came something brilliant, apparently, as it didn't take long for the finished product to appear in Big Apple Magazine. *Heartbreak on the Atlantic Coast* was a sprawling tale of my sorrow and my misadventures, and a studied appreciation of the landscape and the people I encountered along the way. The city folk seemed fascinated by it, by my rural understanding and my urban sensibilities. Not long after, I received an offer to become a staff writer there.

In my terror, certain that I could never produce another article of the same caliber, it had taken a lot of convincing on Ryan's part to get me to accept. With his support, I found that I actually did have more things to write about.

Together we moved our meager belongings into a homely one-bedroom in Queens. It's not very nice, but it's not terrible. There's even laundry in the basement.

I roll onto my side. Ryan is still sleeping, wrapped haphazardly in our thin summer sheets, naked beneath the linen. His forehead wrinkles with the stress that never leaves him, even when he's asleep. The stress of knowing that, in a mere seven days, it's back to graduate school and back to drowning in books and explications of poems. Back to staying late at the library, texting me too much, when he ought to be studying. Back to coming home and falling asleep face-down on the couch with his glasses still on, while I sit awake at our desk, pulling my hair out to try and make something worth reading. Back to one night a week where we actually get to look at each other, and talk, and make up for lost time with our tongues, our teeth, our hands.

And yet we still don't feel like the grown-ups we're supposed to be. We still feel like mischievous kids, ones who have snuck into this building and do not belong there. Like we've conned our way into adulthood. But I've been told it never really feels like you're made it, even when you have. Even when you can pay your rent and you have neighbors that like you.

I wake him up with a kiss to his neck. We have fallen into these little intimate routines. I've been warned that routines can breed contempt and boredom, but it has been three years, and each day still manages to excite me. Maybe it's not the same as it was when we met, maybe I don't feel dizzy in his presence all the time anymore, maybe sometimes I even find myself rolling my eyes at his habits and neuroses. But when I'm at work, when I'm out shopping, whenever I'm away from him, I smile at the thought of coming back home to him. I've never smiled at the prospect of coming home before.

When I left my mother's house, she'd cried. I'm not sure if it was because she would miss me, or if it was because my departure was the final evidence that she'd failed in changing me. Ryan doesn't hear from his parents. Sometimes he cries in my arms, because it is impossible for it not to hurt, even when you're so, so happy to be where you are. I have proven to myself, through this, that love doesn't fix you. It can't make things that happened un-happen, and it can't change people who do not see it at its core, who do not experience its elation for themselves. It can only bolster you. It can carry you through anything, if it's right. And every morning I'm reminded how it's so, *so* right.

He wakes up at my sleepy affection and tosses an arm across my body. I curl into the curve of him, breathing in the scent of sleep, how our sweat in the nighttime can't manage to offend. It only makes me endeared, to know that this bed is something we share. We toss and turn and sweat and dream together, in the same place. Forever, if he'll have me. We've talked about it in vague terms. There have been no ring fittings nor dates set.

The coffee timer clicks into its percolating, and we grin at the knowledge that we'll soon feel awake. The apartment, in its smallness, fills with the warm, full scent of a dark roast, bought from a tiny little corner shop, ground down in our galley kitchen, measured out in careful scoops. There is, finally, some sort of order to my life. There is finally the kind of predictability that doesn't bore.

Ryan fries four eggs in the cast-iron pan. I watch him from the living room, curled on the couch beneath a fleece blanket, watching the way the muscles of his bare back move. He is never not beautiful. On the table there lay magazines, open books, post-it notes of reminders written so vaguely we no longer know what we were trying to remind ourselves of. Beneath the sounds of honking cars and shouting strangers, I listen to him hum.

His voice still holds the deep southern charm, even though he has not been there in years. As always, he permeates his surroundings until it looks like he belongs in them, even if he doesn't quite yet feel like a person who owns a coffee pot or pays a monthly utility bill.

These days, when we go to beaches, we do not have to be so shy. In New York, two men may ride the subway, side-by-side and so close, their heads tilted toward one another, talking quietly as they sweat beneath the faulty air conditioning. No one will pay you any mind. And if they do, and if they're cruel, there is always someone there to defend you. There has been no solidarity until now. There has been nowhere we feel truly safe.

The train shakes on its way out to Far Rockaway, and I adjust the strap of our shared tote bag on my bare shoulder. It is, despite the moderate heat, still the perfect weather for tank tops and flip flops, for not-so-subtle tan lines that first must burn and bubble before they smooth. Our stop comes, and we hold hands all the way through the door, pushing past strangers who just want to get where they are going, who just want to tune out the dirty world around them, even if your limbs must brush against each other's. We're relieved by the cooler air of the platform, even though it still smells like an ancient collection of rain and piss. You get used to it. You almost come to like it. Like a birthmark, or a flaw in a person you love. You know it's bad, but it's yours, so you reserve the right to love it.

The beach is crowded, loud with the splashing and yelling of children clinging desperately to what's left of their freedom. We don't plan to go in the water. Maybe that is something about us that makes us grownups. We don't need to swim and play, even if sometimes, watching the low waves, there's nothing I want more than to stand waist-deep in the water and let it carry me. We want to just sit beneath a pavilion, quietly enjoying one another, and eventually work up the sweat to walk through the surf, leaving footprints that will so swiftly wash away.

The shore stretches out before us. Like a darkened hallway, like a field of corn. This is the ocean we once followed that brought us to our sorrow. If we kept going, walking barefoot down the coast, eventually we would come to the place where I became certain that I would love him forever. To the place where we agreed to take each other to bed, where we touched beneath the water and it made me feel as if no one had ever appreciated the ocean in the way that we did. The ocean became ours. So many places were ours. An abandoned building, a cheap liquor store, a dormitory at a state university. A bus, a train, a Cadillac. A cornfield, an old bed. The world is very much alive with him, with us.

We don't have to walk the entire coast. No one can tell us what we can and cannot do. Not anymore.

We hold hands in the shallow water, our feet slowly buried beneath the wet, heavy sand, as the summer goes on all around us. Even if I were to be stuck here, up to my skinny ankles in sand, it would be a fine way to live. Maybe, for the first time, I could look like Ryan did everywhere. Belonging in a place, looking right.

He notices my dreamy staring, how my eyes trace the geography of the surf as it shrinks into the distance.

"What's wrong, bud?" he asks, tucking a finger beneath my chin, guiding me to face him. I smile my involuntary smile at the sight of him.

"Nothing," I tell him, meaning it. Of course, there are things, there are stressors. My job, my family, his family. Global warming, maybe. There are so many things wrong, but standing in the shallow ocean, it doesn't matter. "Nothing."

We make it all the way to the dilapidated boardwalk and its high grass and its sand mixed with dirt. We don't approach it, knowing that it is nothing but a hotbed of splinters. It is a remnant of the way the city used to be. Ryan says it reminds him of home, how wood seems always wet and dry all at once, how you just can't get rid of the insects that swarm the posts and planks.

Bare-foot weather. We curl our toes into the hot sand.

Sometimes I'm reminded of the waking fear I felt, years ago, while we were apart. I am standing with him in a perfect moment in the sun, and I become afraid that I will wake up once again, alone on a bed, reaching across toward no one. In those moments, I collect him in my arms, at the waist. I grind myself into him and remind myself that I am already awake.